I0595596

Humphry Repton

Variety

A collection of essays

Humphry Repton

Variety
A collection of essays

ISBN/EAN: 9783337218133

Printed in Europe, USA, Canada, Australia, Japan

Cover: Foto ©Andreas Hilbeck / pixelio.de

More available books at **www.hansebooks.com**

V A R I E T Y:

A

COLLECTION OF ESSAYS.

[PRICE THREE SHILLINGS AND SIXPENCE.]

A

COLLECTION OF ESSAYS.

WRITTEN IN THE YEAR 1787.

Tum ut Varietas occurreret Satietati.

CIC. ORAT.

Nullius addictus jurare in verba magistri.

HORAT.

L O N D O N:

PRINTED FOR T. CADELL, IN THE STRAND.

M DCC LXXXVIII.

PREFATORY

ADVERTISEMENT.

THE following Effays were intended to have appeared *periodically*,
but, on confulting their Publifher, the
Authors, who are little verfed in *the art
and myftery of Book-making*, were informed
that the times were fo much altered
fince the WORLD and CONNOISSEUR made
their appearance *weekly*, about 30 years
ago, that any attempt to revive fuch
mode of publications muft now prove
unfuccefsful, fince every Effay would
be hafh'd, or minc'd, if not ferved up

a 3   entire,

entire, in the daily papers like a Mainte-
non Cutlet, as the MIRROR and LOUN-
GER have been cut out into Scotch col-
lops: He therefore advised, either that
the whole stock of provision should be
set before the public at once, or tossed
into the kitchen fire all together.

ON this, the several authors hesitated
a little, modestly supposing, that some
of the papers might perish without injury to mankind; but each individual
could discern so much merit in certain
Essays, *i. e.* of *his own*, that conscience
would not permit him to deprive the
publick of so delicious an entertainment: Thus, at a time when it is the
fashion to print *Tragedies intended to have
been acted*, and *Speeches intended to have
been spoken*, they have resolved to print
these *Periodical Papers intended to have
been published* WEEKLY.

ALL

ALL writers are fond of allusions to good eating, (perhaps becaufe they frequently confider a good dinner as the *fummum bonum* of all happinefs; or, perhaps, becaufe men generally think moft of that which they moft feldom enjoy) however this may be, the hackneyed culinary fimile muft ftill be ufed to give fome further account of this little volume.

THE entertainment of which you are invited to partake (paying 3 s. 6 d. for your ticket) is neither a *plain family dinner*, nor a *fplendid city feaft*, but rather what the French call *un petit foupé*, confifting of VARIETY of difhes, chiefly light and eafy of digeftion: fhould there indeed be fome, compofed of more folid materials; the ham and beef are fcraped delicately, or cut in very thin flices—to this repaft all are welcome,

except

except thofe profeffed Authors, who fancy they keep a better table at home, and thofe profeffed criticks who go abroad only to find fault.

THE invitation cannot be better worded than in three lines of the Prologue to Congreve's *Love for Love.*

" We hope there's fomething that may pleafe
    each tafte,
" And, tho' of homely fare we make the feaft,
" Yet you will find VARIETY at leaft."

CON-

CONTENTS.

CONTENTS.

XXI. Out-

CONTENTS.

VARIETY.

NUMBER I.

" I AM going to tell you a ftory that will make you all laugh." Who has not heard of George Alexander Steevens? A man of excellent humour, and whofe wit and mimickry has often kept an audience in continual laughter. He declared that the manner in which I have begun this Effay, is the moft impolitic of all poffible ways of beginning to tell a ftory. And yet many will confider the title prefixed to my paper in the fame light, and conftrue it into an engagement of more than I fhall be able to perform, or at leaft predict a fpeedy termination to my labours. For who can promife

to

to fupply Variety long in thefe faftidious
times ? Readers of every denomination will
fneer at fo bold a title, and I already anticipate the contemptuous exclamation of fome
furly critick, who, taking up this paper, perhaps will cry out, " Variety!　And who
" dares hope to furnifh this in the beaten track
" of periodical effay-writing ?　Has not
" the Spectator told us all he faw ?　The
" Tatler all he heard ?　The Guardian
" all he thought ?　The Connoisseur all he
" knew ?　And the Adventurer all he met
" with ?　Has not Fitzadam, full thirty years
" ago, faid all the witty things that could be
" faid in the World? Nay, farther, has not
" the mighty Rambler, with folid argu-
" ments and nervous ftile, compleatly filled
" the meafure of Variety, by leaving no-
" thing new to fay?"　But here I muft ftop
my critic, by obferving that it is *Variety* I
promife, and not *Novelty :* for one Solomon,
a very learned Effay-writer among the Jews,
declared about two thoufand years ago,
that, " there was nothing new under the
" fun,"—By which I fuppofe he meant,
that lunaticks, or thofe under the moon, are
the only people who can hope to find novelty. Since men with found underftandings,
improved

improved by experience, and cultivated by much reading, will perceive a famenefs in the writers of every age, and laugh at all attempts to produce even an Effay or an Apothegm, which has not before been ferved up to the public.

Moft of my predeceffors have given fome account of themfelves and their defign in their firft Effay, and therefore, for Variety's fake, I ought to leave you in the dark with refpect to both. I will not difappoint you, but in compliance with cuftom and my reader's curiofity, my firft number fhall give fome account of the firft perfon in my good opinion ; for to adopt a familiar phrafe, " who is it that does not think well of num- " ber one ?" Know then, all ye, who pant for a new acquaintance, that the author of Variety is a gentleman, that he is called Walter Weathercock, Efq; of a very refpectable family in the county of ——, in his fortune he is comfortably eafy, rather than fplendidly affluent, too rich to be a rafcal from neceffity, too poor to become one from ambition, and too honeft to allow any plea fufficient for being one at all : an early thirft for Variety, induced him by travel to add a knowledge of modern laws and manners, to thofe of the ancients, which he had learnt in the public fchools; his reading has been general, and in many different languages, for though he is neither able to conftrue the Alkoran, nor to hold a converfation in Cherokee; he has had *French* frizzed into his head with marechal powder; *Italian* flips off his tongue like macaroni; and he has taken in the *high German* Gutterals with the old Hock of the country; as to *Latin* and *Greek* they were early driven into him by the ufual channels; for thefe being fundamental to all other learning, and yet having a natural tendeney to rife. It has always been the cuftom at public fchools, to inftill the dead languages into a part where no living tongue ever exifts, and as far as poffible from the feat of the mother tongue; and yet notwithftanding this wife precaution, 'tis wonderful with what alacrity they mount from the tail to the head, and overpower every other fpecies of learning. This is vifible from the fchool-boy, who quotes fcraps of *Latin* in the holidays, to the profound claffic, who defpifes every thing that is not *Greek*. The author's companions are men of fafhion, and men of pleafure, men of feeling, and men of literature, men of bufi-

nefs,

nefs, and women of every defcription ; but as
an ardent love of Variety will not permit
men or books to fill up all the vacuities
of a reftlefs active mind, unoccupied by daily
employment ; he can *fiddle* with the muſician,
ſketch with the painter, and *play a rubber*
or *drink a bottle* with thoſe who can do nothing
elfe.   In ſhort, he is not aſhamed to mix with
folly where 'tis innocent, nor afraid to join
the world where 'tis not diſhonourable ; always preferring mirth to ſadnefs, and convinced that one day of cheerfulnefs is better
than a whole month of ſorrow.   He divides
his time betwixt the town and country, feek-
ing Variety in the court, and in the cottage ; yet often finding famenefs of buftle, in
the mafquerade, or the village fair ; and
famenefs of folitude in the retired coverts of a
foreft, or the ſnug corner of a box in a
public coffee-room.   Having thus introduced
myfelf in the third perfon, (which by the bye,
is a modeft *variety* of egotifm) you will fancy you know me whenever we meet, and will
pronounce a famenefs in my ftile, but do not
rifque your judgment too haftily, for I ſhall
often give you as my own, the thoughts of
perfons, more lively, or more learned than
myfelf, who have agreed to join their powers

in the arduous tafk of furnifhing *Variety*, a
tafk in which no individual, however verfa-
tile his abilities, or defultory his purfuits,
can long hope to engage the world's attention.
I am fingled out like the youngeft council
from amongft a very able groupe, to open the
defign of this new periodical publication, and
to become the Editor. In this character, I am
inftructed by my brief to fay, that I fhall not
only follow the example of my predeceffors,
in publifhing fuch Effays as I think deferve
attention, but I will ftill go farther; I will
follicit the correfpondence of all fuch as fancy
their own productions *do* deferve it, and fhould
the partiality of the parent at any time exceed
the merits of his offspring, the bantling
fhall not be fmothered in contemptuous
filence, or the fond father's hopes be blafted
by malicious criticifm. But each objecti-
onable Effay, fhall be noticed or returned,
with reafons for its non-appearance, dictated
by candour, and delivered with tendernefs.   Under fuch regulations, this paper
may become the fofter-mother of early genius,
and the nurfe of bafhful merit, where thofe
who have *much leifure* may convey their own
thoughts to the public in their own manner, and thofe who have *little leifure* may fee
                                                    their

their flighteft hints noticed, enlarged, digeft-
ed, or improved.

Should this invitation call forth all the
latent aid that hope fuggefts, *Variety* will not
appear too promifing a title for a work,
where fubjects of every defcription fhall find
a place, but it may be neceffary to obferve,
that although allufions to *religion* and *politics*
may be occafionally admiffible, yet fhould
whole Effays on thofe fubjects be frequently
inferted, all *Variety* would foon be loft in the
feuds of party, or the difputations of contro-
verfial jargon; befides, they are matters fo generally underftood, and fo perfectly adapted to
the meaneft capacity, that every attempt
to throw light, or produce Variety on thefe
fubjects, would be prefumptuous and uninterefting.

As it is common with a Tranflator to extoll
the merits of his original, and of an Hiftorian
or Biographer to intereft us in the character of
his hero, fo I hope the Effayift may be allowed to magnify the importance of his title,
which I fhall do by this formal addrefs; and
firft to the ladies, *whom* I hope very little
is neceffary to convince how delightful is
Variety. Should any dull beau endeavour to
depreciate its merits in your eyes, reflect on

the

the burthen of an old ſong, which ſays,
" Variety is charming," and be upon your
guard againſt the deſigns of the man who has
not honeſty to confeſs it. To gentlemen, (by
which title is now underſtood all who can
read) I ſhall in few words obſerve of Variety,
that it is inexhauſtible, indeſcribable, and
all comprehenſive, that it pervades all nature
is viſible in every ſpecies of created beings,
and the great ſource of felicity to all rational
ones, (nay I think I could prove on ſome future occaſion, what at firſt view may appear paradoxical) *that in a ſolicitous demand for
Variety, conſiſts the chief and almoſt only diſtinction betwixt men and brutes.* And now, who
that can afford to pay two pence a week, will
not aſſert the dignity of his nature, by contri-
buting to increaſe the demand for Variety ?

   The reader will perceive, that this paper, as well as
thoſe which follow, have not been altered, in conſequence of their being publiſhed all together.

NUMBER

N U M B E R II.

TO fay, " *that the chief and almoſt only diſ-*
" *tinction betwixt Man and Brute, con-*
" *ſiſts in a ſolicitous demand for* VARIETY,"
appears ſo bold an aſſertion, that I can readily
conceive the effect it has on various claſſes of
my readers ; poſſibly in deſcribing their ſeveral comments, I may afford ſome *amuſement* ;
as for *inſtruction*, even vanity will not let me
hope, that my feeble efforts can contribute
to enlarge the ideas of this enlightened
age.   Formerly, indeed, inſtruction and
anruſement went hand in hand.

" *Utile Dulci.—Lectorem delectando, pariterque*
" *monendo.*"

But now, inſtruction is uſeleſs ; we know
every thing by intuition ; a phiſiognomiſt will
read a character in an eye-brow ; and a critick is acquainted with all the ſubject of
a book, from a title page ; but ſhould idleneſs

or curiosity tempt him to read the preface, he becomes so well acquainted with an author's stile and design, that he can write a critique on his work without cutting open the leaves. I shall proceed, therefore, to deliver the various opinions of my readers on the paradox which finishes my first Number. The *Logician* perceives a want of precision in my postulatum; and lays down the paper with contempt, as too trifling for his consideration. The *Lawyer* catches at the word *almost*; considers it as a loophole for the author to creep out, and foresees the matter will never come to an issue, but will be shuffled off by a *nolo prosequi*. The *Divine* predicts heresy and scepticism in every word, and trembles for the soul of man which seems in danger of being lost in VARIETY. The *Politician* cannot perceive how VARIETY can be made the vehicle of his pursuits, when consolidation of customs, simplifying the revenues, and aggregating the funds, seem to hold forth no hope of *change*; and the only symptom of VARIETY, or mutation, has been a commutation of taxes, changing delight for a dish of tea. There is a class of readers, by far the most numerous, who belong to no profession, espouse no party, form no conjectures,

and

and deliver no opinions : in fhort, thofe idle,
lounging, infipid beings, who having learned
to read, but not to employ themfelves,
will occafionally kill time, by fauntering
through a paper, without knowing on what
it treats : the quantity only is what thefe
men regard : they take up a paper, becaufe it
appears fhort ; and if they ever utter any
thing at all about it, it is a complaint,
that it was not longer ; becaufe having finifhed reading it, they are at a lofs what to
do next : for the ufe and convenience of fuch
readers, I have defired my printer to leave
a broad margin ; that fhould the implements
of writing chance to be within reach,
they may divert themfelves with fcrawling
odd figures, or trying a pen ; that fo, the
hand may be employed while the *head* is
vacant.   I have now to defcribe the fentiments of my female readers ; and yet,
I doubt in the multitude of their avocations,
few have had leifure to read more than
the title ; but fhould the captivating appearance of VARIETY, have induced any
one to read a page, while Monfieur Toupee is
putting her fweet treffes in papillots, I fear
fhe may have been retailing my paper to him
during the operation ; and that his demand

B 5

for

for Variety in *shreds*, will have confumed
the whole, before his miſtreſs has come to the
final paragraph ; for her uſe, therefore, I begin this number by the aſſertion with which
I concluded my laſt ; and I think I perceive
her ſtruck with the juſtneſs of the remark,
and repeating theſe words : " Variety ! in-
" deed ! and is that the only diſtinction
" betwixt Men and Brutes ?   Upon my
" word, I'm half inclined to think, there's
" no diſtinction at all ; or certainly, if there
" be any, this author is right, it muſt be in
" proportion to their ability of furniſhing us
" with dear Variety." There is another ſort
of readers, whoſe comments claim ſome notice, although they may not deſerve any :
theſe are the cavillers ;   the jaundice eyed
fault-finders : in ſhort, prating critics of every
deſcription, whether from profeſſion, from
idleneſs, from vanity, or from malice ; who,
like the *inſects* on our peach trees, eagerly fix
on the firſt leaf they perceive, ſhrivel up its
ſurface, deform its beauties, and blaſt the
hope of future fruit. I will anticipate the
malice of theſe fell-deſtroyers, by putting
words into their mouths. Let one ſay, " the
" work is beneath all criticiſm ;" another,
that " it abounds with ſo much abſurdity, he

" knows

" knows not where to begin the attack ;"
a third, yawning, may folemnly pronounce the
fimple word, " dull;" a fourth, condefcend-
ing to be more particular, may declare, that
" it attempts wit without occafion, and hu-
" mour without effect ;" a fifth ftill more
particular, very confequentially obferves,
" that the ftile is incorrect; the manner
" affected; the matter uninterefting, and
" the fubjects will be trite."   To all this I
have but one anfwer: Gentlemen! if you
don't like one number, take another; for
every one fhall contain Variety.

IT was an obfervation of Pliny the elder,
" that he never read a book from which he
" could not derive fome advantage ;" fo poffibly the following anecdote of myfelf, and
four of my countrymen, may be of ufe to the
extenfive clafs of cavillers. We fat out together from Hamburg, to crofs the comfortlefs
and dreary fands of Weftphalia.   During the
firft day's journey, each indulged the right of
complaining, with all the virulence of Englifh prejudice, heightened by the inconveniencies of travelling through a foreign country.
The roads were villainous; the horfes raf-
cally; the carriage infamous; and, having
expended all human epithets of reproach on
thefe

thefe, the drivers and innkeepers, were infer-
nal and diabolical.   In fhort, fo compleatly
were we diffatisfied, deranged, and out of humour with every thing we faw in the day,
that our evening was fretful, quarrelfome,
and tedious amongft ourfelves, till it was
fortunately propofed by one of the company,
to try an experiment the following day;
which was fimply this : that every one fhould
affect to be moft pleafed, when he was really
moft difgufted ; and that no one fhould utter
a complaint under the penalty of defraying
the day's expences. We all readily confented,
though poffibly from various motives ; fome
impelled by the hope of catching their companions tripping ; and others, (like myfelf)
hoping it might afford Variety, by changing
ufelefs complaints, to ironical panegyric.
Full of this intended reformation, we rofe
early next morning ; the fun fhone brightly
on our defign, and added ftrength to our re-
folutions : (elfe, being all Englifhmen, a
cloudy day might have deftroyed the whole
plan) the fandy roads became turnpikes ; the
horfes, Englifh hunters ; the poft-waggon,
a landau ; and the dreary plains, a fertile
country ; every thing was commended hyper-
bolically ; till even execrable bacon, and half

hatch'd

hatch'd eggs, were recommended as Weftphalia ham, and early fpring chickens: by
being thus gradually accuftomed to be pleafant under difficulties, and laugh at hardfhips
inftead of complaining, we became fatisfied
with our accommodations, and in good humour with ourfelves, and one another.   Indeed, fo much reafon had I to be pleafed with
its effect, that I determined, as far as poffible,
to follow the fame chearful habit in my journey through life; and, when difappointment, or misfortune, have attempted to affail
me, I can fmile at their attack, and call them
bleffings.   To the good natured man, my
ftory will need no application; and, if the
fullen critic finds enjoyment, in complaining
that my work is dull, I cannot help it, at leaft
it will afford me Variety in the means of giving delight.   To pleafe all, by every Effay, is
impoffible; but to amufe fome, by every attempt, is probable; and therefore, the attempt
is laudable.

P. S.   While thefe papers appeared feparately, the
occafional criticifms might aptly be compared to blights
or infects attacking the early leaves; but being now
grown up into a volume, they are become expofed to
more lafting comments, from criticks of a higher order.
REVIEWERS may be confidered as nurfery-men and
gardeners,

gardeners, who, though they sometimes haſtily deſtroy a harmleſs flower in their monthly labours, to root out noxious weeds; yet, often by tranſplanting cuttings to their eſtabliſhed garden, they have preſerved and reared a ſickly plant; or one, whoſe diminutive growth, without ſuch aſſiſtance, could not have made its way in the prolific crouded ſoil of literature. If, from this little ſhrub, theſe Gardeners can ſelect a noſegay,—they are welcome;—but let them not gather only faded flowers, and withered leaves, to ſhew the tree is barren; —nor cut a ſwitch, to flog the authors, and ſay, there is not a ſingle ſhoot to make a decent riding ſtick for Amuſement; or on which Morality may, walking, lean with ſafety.

N U M B E R   III.

A FEW nights ago, after coming from the Theatre, where a new piece had proved unfuccefsful; or, in the common phrafe, had been *damned by the town*, I could not help reflecting on the mortification which its author muft that night feel; and this naturally leading me to recall the occafional difappointments I had myfelf experienced, my activity became gradually oppreffed, and I infenfibly funk into a trance, which fo engroffed my mind, that at this moment I can fcarce determine, whether I was awake or not.   The vifion was too much connected to appear a dream, and I have not fufficient faith in modern miracles, to think I was awake.   My candles gradually loft their brightnefs, and at length caft fo faint a gleam, that I could hardly diftinguifh what I am about to tell.   But, methought, an airy

phantom

phantom ftood before me, her veft was unlike in fabrick, fhape or colour, to any thing
on earth; her flowing robe was of the moft
perfect white; a lofty plume of feathers graced
her head; her face was covered by a veil,
through which it only half appeared; and
in her-hand fhe held a parchment book.
While I was gazing with terror and furprize,
and hefitated whether it portended good
or evil, the heavenly form addreffed me
thus: " Fear nothing; behold! before thee
" ftands the parent of invention, and the
" celeftial patron of *Variety*; my name is
" FANCY; I am fent by that power at
" whofe command I fill the foul of genius,
" to reveal to thee, the facred book of myftic
" *Allegory*, from whence thou art permit-
" ted to tranfcribe that *page* which tells the
" *hiftory of* HOPE *and* EXPECTATION; quickly
" perform the tafk which thou art fet, and
" fail not to employ the lucky moment
" which FANCY recommends, to furnifh more
" *Variety*." So faying, fhe laid the book
upon my defk and vanifhed; while I affidu-
oufly fat down and copied from the open
page as follows. "HOPE is the favourite fon
" of *heavenly benevolence*, whofe charms none
" that fee them can refift, and the brightnefs
" of

" of whofe countenance can cheer the
" gloomy horrors of a dungeon with a fmile ;
" to him was given from the foundation
" of the world a fpoufe unlike himfelf, her
" name was FEAR, the daughter of GUILT.
" Why beauty became thus coupled with
" deformity, prefume not to enquire, nor
" dare to fcan the purpofes of everlafting
" wifdom, or meafure its refolves by the con-
" tracted fcale of human underftanding, but
" what thou feeft written, let thy pen with
" faithfulnefs record. Jointly to HOPE and
" FEAR was given dominion over all man-
" kind, and from their hateful union fprang
" two fickly children; DOUBT, which totter-
" ed as he walked by HOPE, and ANXIETY,
" trembling by the fide of FEAR. Mutual dif-
" guft foon rendered it impoffible for HOPE
" and FEAR to dwell together, and at length
" in pity to the excellence of HOPE, a fepa-
" ration from his fpoufe was granted by the
" Fates, and their dominion over mortals
" was divided and alternate. The bonds of
" this detefted marriage being cancelled,
" licence was given to HOPE to feek another
" bride, that he might re-produce his virtues
" with his fpecies. HOPE then became at-
" tached to PROBABILITY, a fimple maid,
" whofe

" whofe willing manner tempted his ad-
" dreffes.   She was eafy of accefs, and the
" light veil which covered all her charms,
" became tranfparent to the glowing eye
" of Hòpe, his amorous foul kindled with
" fond defire, and from their warm em-
" braces fprang a daughter named Success,
" who foon became the darling of her father,
" and he affigned for her attendants, *Joy* and
" *Happinefs*. Probability had an only fifter,
" who refembled her in every grace and fea-
" ture, her name was Possibility ; indeed
" the likenefs was fo ftrong, that even Hope
" himfelf would not always have been able
" to diftinguifh them afunder, but for the
" armour of *Difficulty*, which was the
" conftant garb of Possibility. Hope, ever
" eager in his temper, one evening difcover-
" ed this fifter of his new-made fpoufe, naked
" and alone ; he rufhed towards her with ar-
" dor not to be repreffed, miftook her perfon,
" and fhe, *uncloathed* and *defencelefs*, yielded to
" his embrace. Hope was too fervent to dif-
" cern, that inftead of Probability, he had
" taken to his arms *bare* Possibility. From
" this inceftuous miftake, two fifter twins
" were born, but fo unlike each other that
" it was fcarcely credible fuch different
" children

" children could have proceeded from one
" fource; the elder of thefe two, from fome
" refemblance to her father, they called Ex-
" PECTATION ; her infancy was highly pro-
" mifing, and as fhe grew up, her natural
" impetuofity of temper, was checked by *Pa-*
" *tience*, and her legitimate brothers DOUBT
" and ANXIETY, having become her chief
" companions, fhe was not a ftranger to her fa-
" ther's former wife; thus FEAR was at times
" admitted, tho' fhe never was a friend.
" The other twin was called DISAPPOINT-
" MENT, an execrable wretch, the curfe of all
" who knew her, ugly and deformed in per-
" fon, and loathfome in her manners; her fa-
" ther-fickened when he looked upon her,
" and her fifter trembled at her bare ap-
" proach, fhe knew neither *Joy* nor *Hap-*
" *pinefs*, but was the fworn ally of *Mifery*
" and *Grief*, with all their curfed attendants
" of *woe* and *forrow*, *anguifh* and *regret*, and
" *bitternefs* of *thought*. With thefe fhe would
" folace in cups of *envy*, or ftupify her fenfes
" with the waters of *defpair*, fhe was fhunned
" by all the world except her father, who
" would fometimes ftrive, though often in
" vain, to draw her from this melancholy
" crew, yet fhe feldom liftened to the call of
                                        HOPE.

" Hope. She hated all the favourites of
" Success, and often dared to break upon her
" sister's slumbers, and disturb the pleasing
" dreams of Expectation, and though she
" knew her sister dreaded her pursuit, she ne-
" ver ceased to persecute and follow her: when
" Expectation promised to her votaries the
" smiling patronage of well deserved Suc-
" cess, she would snatch them from his power
" and spread her baneful influence round
" them, till beset by her associates *Grief* and
" *Vexation*, they would drink with her the
" maddening waters of *Despair*. A draught of
" this will chill the spirit of exertion, and
" those who taste it become the servants of
" Neglect, a powerful hag, whose dark and
" dismal cave is ——."
. I had transcribed so far, and was about to
turn over the following page, when Fancy
again appeared, and holding back my hand,
she said, Stop there! proceed no farther, *Va-*
" *riety* must not look forward to *Neglect*, it is
" enough for thee that thou art not a stranger
" to the power of *Disappointment*. Write,
" therefore, to the sons of men, tell them,
" that none can know the pleasures of *Success*,
" who have not been first led by *Expectation*;
" yet let them beware how far they trust her
" specious

" fpecious promifes, let them not prefume on
" the fupport of *Merit, Induftry*, or *Good In-*
" *tentions*, for thefe cannot defend againft the
" wiles of *Difappointment*, ever watching to
" betray the votaries of her fifter to *Grief*
" and four *Vexation*.   From the cruel gripe
" of thefe, HOPE may yet deliver them,
" but after men become familiar with their
" dull fociety, and tafte the waters of *Defpair*,
" HOPE can no longer fave, and they are loft
" for ever to the world and to themfelves."
So faying, FANCY vanifhed, not on a fudden as
before, but gradually diminifhed in my fight,
the fnowy whitenefs of her robe became
tranfparent, and folds that loofely waved in
the wind became a hollow mafs of chryftal,
through which I faw her wonderous form dif-
folve into a fluid, changing its colour like the
rays of light; firft it appeared like blood, then
melted into liquid gold, then 'twas an
emerald diffolved, from green it changed to
blue, from blue to purple, and at length it
deepened to a perfect black, the lofty plumes
were feathers ftill, but they no longer nodded
on the phantom's head, their ftems were
dipped into the fluid, and the whole at length
affumed the well known fhape of *imple-*
ments for writing. When I was recovered
from

from the confternation into which this gradual metamorphofis had thrown me, I looked
for the volume whence I had tranfcribed the
hiftory of HOPE and EXPECTATION; but behold, inftead of it there lay open before me a
little printed book, I think it was a volume
of Pope's Letters, in which the following
paffage caught my eye, " *Bleſſed is he who ex-*
" *pecteth nothing: for he ſhall never be diſ-*
" *appointed.*"   Vexed to perceive that it was
all illufion, I dafhed the little volume from
my defk, and ringing for my flippers, retired
to reft.

NUM.

N U M B E R IV.

***

IT has often been matter of doubt, whether
Moral Precepts may be more ftrongly in-
culcated by an appeal to the *underftanding*, or
to the *paffions* : in other words, whether the
head, or heart of man fhould be addreffed to
infpire virtuous, or correct vicious inclinations ; but it is from not duly confidering the
infinite variety of individual difpofitions, that
fuch doubts can ever have arifen. The
teachers of mankind are too apt to imagine,
that the fame mode of inftruction which has
operated on fome, may be effective towards
all ; and feldom reflect on that infinite diver-
fity, of temperament and character which di-
ftinguifhes every man from thofe who moft
nearly feem to refemble him. I am led to the
confideration of this fubject, by frequent obfervations on the oppofite characters of my

two intimate friends Harry and Tom * * ;
they are brothers, and refemble each other in
fome particulars, yet are as different in
others, as heat from cold, or any extremes in
nature; they are both men of excellent underftandings, of liberal education, and generous
difpofitions; they both received their rudi-
ments of knowledge at the fame fchool, and
under the fame tutors; yet muft they be
moved to the exertion of their amiable characters, by very different motives. Harry,
whether, from a natural coldnefs of heart, or
from having occafionally fuffered by impofi-
tion, is flow and cautious how he gives credit
to tales of diftrefs, or relief to objects of compaffion; yet, does he never refufe his ampleft
contributions to alleviate calamity well authenticated, and never withholds his vigorous
fupport to public charities, well recommended: he is a man of bufinefs, without having
any thing to do; becaufe, the flighteft occur-
rence muft be ferioufly confidered, and every
trifling event becomes the fubject of earneft
difquifition.   The impromptu of wit never
reaches Harry, and ridicule is hardly underftood by him; his converfation is matter
of fact, with abftrufe reafoning on every
topic; and his mind has, by long ufe, acquired.

qnired, what he calls a habit of generalising his ideas on every fubject. His reading, is what moft would call dry, and requires the deepeft attention : he has often declared, that he could never derive the fmalleft entertainment from the perufal of a novel, a tale, or even a dramatic performance. Tom, on the contrary, is the flave of fudden emotion; and his life is a continued feries of beneficent intentions; yet is he for ever, difappointing the hopes of thofe who look to him for affiftance. To know diftrefs, and to relieve it, are with him the effect of the fame inftant, wherever it is poffible; but a paufe weakens the impulfe of his generofity, and the effence of his benevolence, evaporates by delay.

I will difplay my friends' characters by fome inftances of their life, to which I have been a witnefs. A few days ago, I accompanied thefe two brothers, to vifit the cells of a new county prifon, in which convicts are punifhed by folitary confinement, and continual labour; amongft the feveral objects that called our attention, we were particularly ftruck with one: it was a female figure, of an elegant form, middle aged, and a fwarthy complexion, fitting on the corner of her bed; fhe was neat and plainly dreffed, and was fill-

ing

ing up a part of that single hour in the day which is allowed from the labours of spinning, by mending a hole in a clean white stocking; she had been six months confined in this lonesome habitation, without seeing or conversing with any living creature, but the keeper of the prison, or his surly deputy: at the first removal of the slider in the door, thro' which we viewed her, she looked up with an expressive eye of grief and surprise to see herself the object of curiosity; and then, with an air of melancholy indifference, returned to her task, with her needle; struck with her appearance, we asked the cause of her commitment: the keeper said she was a fortune-teller, and dealt with the devil; but she interrupted his answer, by saying, she was a-gipsey, who was sentenced to twelve months solitary imprisonment within those walls, for having practised her trade of foretelling future events. "Then" says my friend Harry, "you pretend to be acquainted with "whatever will happen." "That, Sir," said she, "is part of our profession." Tom observed, that he supposed she hardly looked forward to the sentence under which she was suffering. She replied with a half smile, accompanied by a tear; "if you will survey the narrow

" narrow compafs to which I am confined,
" you muſt allow, Sir, that a year is a long
" time to look forward." Whether my
friend's paſſions were moved by the repartee
itſelf, or by the look, tone, or manner
in which it was delivered, I cannot tell; but,
turning from the door, he wiped a tear from
his eye, and ſwore he would do ſomething towards relieving the charming woman, while
Harry was aſtoniſhed at what his brother
could be ſo much affected with. We then en-
quired of the keeper, the nature of her crime;
which he told us, was ſimply this: that on
being aſked by a poor credulous girl, what
huſband ſhe ſhould have, the gipſey perſuaded
her to leave her gown and cloak, that
ſhe might lay them under her pillow, and
dream an anſwer to her enquiries; and that
when ſhe had dreamt of the man, ſhe would
return the cloaths; but either the gipſey
could not ſleep; or ſlept, and could not
dream; and the cloaths were never returned
till the law ſet them at liberty, and doomed
the propheteſs to an impriſonment, which *ſhe*
had never dreamt of. Tom was delighted
with the girl's ingenuity, and reſolved moſt
fervently to appear in her favour, and plead

C 3

her

her cause himself. Harry insisted, that it was a palpable fraud, and that she was justly punished. Tom defended her wit, and praised her person. Harry denied, that they were any arguments in her favour; and, after a few days, Tom agreed in his opinion, that the gipsey was an artful baggage, who had not the smallest claim to his compassion.

On another occasion, returning late thro' the Strand, from our club, with Harry and Tom, we observed some bustle in an adjoining street; Tom was eager to enquire the cause; but Harry advised, that we should push forward, lest we might be drawn into difficulties that did not concern us; and urged some prudential arguments for taking his advice. The shrieks of a female in distress, had more effect on Tom; he instantly sprang from us to the place, and discovered, that an innocent servant maid, had been rescued from the brutal attack of a drunken libertine, by a gentleman who was accidentally passing by: before we came up with them, the watch had been alarmed; and we found Tom, with great vehemence, execrating these vigilant preservers of the peace by night: for they had suffered the intoxicated offender to escape, and were extorting money from the poor

poor girl, and her deliverer, by threatning to convey them both to the watch-house. Tom recommended them to submit, and pledged himself to appear as an evidence against these harpies of nocturnal justice. We all gave in our names to appear against the conſtables, who defied us with *inſolence of office*; and we proceeded on our way, amidſt the obſervations of Harry, on the trouble this might occaſion, and the triumph of Tom, in the proſpect of bringing to puniſhment, ſuch enormity and injuſtice. Some time paſſed before we were called upon to appear in behalf of the gentleman; when Tom's ardours had grown cool; and he declared he could not ſufficiently recollect the circumſtances of the event; feared he ſhould expoſe himſelf by ſpeaking to it in public; and, at length abſolutely determined not to go : nor could any arguments of Harry, and myſelf, induce him to compleat an act of duty, which no argument could diſſuade him from originally commencing. The ſtrangers, however, obtained juſtice; and the offenders were puniſhed from our evidence; but not in ſo ample a manner, as might have been effected, had Tom declared the circumſtances with that energy of reſent-

ment

ment which he felt at the moment when he advised the gentleman to prosecute.

FROM hence, I would deduce, that such men as Tom, are only to be moved, by appealing to the passions; and such as Harry, by solid argument; and that those who commend only, in moral Essays, the stile of Sherlock, Tillotson, or Locke, on one side; or, of Sterne, Swift, and Fielding, on the other; are equally as absurd as those who object to every thing, either sweet or sour: both are occasionally good; perhaps best, when properly blended; but certainly, different palates will require, that either one or the other should, in a degree, predominate.

N U M B E R V.

Although the firft of the following letters is a point blank attack, and the other a random one, upon the effects of this work, I fhall publifh both without alteration, to convince the public of my impartiality.

Mr. W E A T H E R C O C K.

S I R,

I LOOK upon it that you are going to make much mifchief, and that makes good what all the world knows, that people who have nothing to do, never do good. I am a hard working Cabinet-maker, and a mafter workman in a fmall way, for I fcorn to work as journeyman to any one. And fo when

I began the world, I laid out all my little fortune in mahogany; but juſt as I had wrought it into tea tables, caddies, fire ſcreens, and bottle ſliders, behold nothing would go down but your inlaid gimcracks. What was to be done? I ſold off all my ſtock for the value of the materials, bought ebony, holly, hiccory, and air-wood, and ſet myſelf to work again. But I had hardly finiſhed an aſſortment before they rendered all my articles unſaleable, by making chairs and tables of paper, painted like ſnuff-boxes and picktooth cafes. Now, all this comes of folks being mad after Variety; and you come and tell us, that 'tis all natural and as it ſhould be: Why at this rate, a man will never know when he has learned a buſineſs that he may get his living by. It was not ſo in Queen Elizabeth's days, for I have heard ſhe uſed to ſay, *ſemper eadem*, which they tell me is Latin for " no Variety," and that's what I'm for. And ſo no more at preſent from

Your humble ſervant,

OLIVER SELFSAME,

Mr.

Mr. Weathercock.

SIR,

I AM possessed of a good fortune, acquired by my father, who was of French extraction, and a wit; for he used to say, that a man who had a French name, had one thing requisite towards getting money, whether he makes the head or the body of man his chief object; that is, whether he become a pastry-cook or a perriwig-maker, a teacher of languages or a taylor. And so my father retired from business with ten thousand pounds, by making short coats and long bills; and while half the admired coxcombs owed him money, they also owed him every thing for which they were admired. I being an only son, and my father a sickly man, he wished to see me well married before he died, and this wish was accomplished exactly. I'll tell you how it happened:—An Irish Knight (who was deep in his books) having been killed in a duel, my father waited on the widow, and scarce had he fixed his eyes on her stately person, but he resolved to embrace the opportunity of raising the consequence of our family

by

by fuch a connection; and indeed it was in
fome danger of dwindling into dwarfifh infignificance, for my father was but five feet high,
and he was taller by a head than me.   Now,
the widow of Sir Phelim O'Ballabruch Mac
Callaghan, my fublime and lofty wife, mea-
fures fix feet three inches without her fhoes,
No great perfuafion was neceffary to fettle
matters betwixt us, and her Ladyfhip confented to accept of my fortune, and *little
me* into the bargain.   i will not trouble you
with the feafting and joy with which our
nuptials were celebrated, for it coft me
the life of my father, as i before told you he
was of a delicate frame ; on this occafion his
wit and his wine flowed in great abundance.
Now, whether it was the falt of his wit, the
ftrength of his wine, or the drynefs of his
jokes, that produced an unufual thirft, I
know not ; but he drank a whole bottle, which
brought on a fever, and he fell a facrifice to
the joy of feeing me fo greatly matched before the firft week of my probation was
expired, leaving me in poffeffion of a large
fortune, and a large wife in poffeffion of
me. During the honey moon my fond fpoufe
difcovered that i was not well, though i was
able to eat, drink and fleep, as well as ever i
                                            did

did in my life; but she knew better, and proposed a journey to Bath; i did all i could to
stay at home; my Lady was not satisfied with
my arguments, indeed i had little to offer; i
had no business but to get in outstanding trifles, and her Ladyship knew i had got in all
i could; in proportion as I shrunk from her
proposal, she grew more desirous; consider
my situation, Sir, she a great body, i hardly
any body; it was in vain for me to think of
pushing things to extremities, and so to Bath
we went. Here her cousin, Captain O'Bryan,
soon found us out, introduced himself to my
Lady, and is become so great a favourite,
that she can't live without him. He is a man
of prodigious parts, as my wife tells me,
though he takes care to hide them from me;
for except that he is as tall as her Ladyship,
i can discover nothing that should make
her prefer his company to mine; nor can
i conceive the motive for her conduct, except
it be Variety; for the Captain and i are
as unlike each other, as broad cloth and
penny binding; i am all meekness, HE all
bluster; i am timid as a flea, HE bold as a turkey cock; i willing to draw myself out of all
contention, HE ready to drive matters to
the utmost; and when my wife appeals to him

in our family concerns, he ftands ftifly to his
opinion, whilft fhe can wind me round
her finger; all this makes me very uneafy at
times, for he often vexes my Lady wife,
and fometimes leaves the houfe a whole day
in a tiff, threatening never to return. i dare
not take her part while he is prefent; yet if i
attempt to do it when we are alone, fhe wonders at my prefumption, and fneers at my infignificance, by inviduous comparifons; i
ftrive to avoid difpleafing her, but can never
do any thing to pleafe her; and if i muft
maintain this great coufin for her Ladyfhip's
fake, furely he ought not to be the fource of
difguft in *her* towards me; when i pity her
for the brutality of his behaviour, fhe tells me
'tis her whim to like it; 'tis VARIETY: and
when i compare my conftant fubmiffion with
his occafional overbearance, fhe tells me that
Variety conftitutes the difference betwixt
man and brute, and bids me read what you
have written; i have done fo; and as you
feem willing to receive all letters, and to
make them fit to fhew themfelves abroad,
i will thank you to drefs up mine in your own
language, fo that my wife may fee it without
knowing it to be a child of my brain; and inform her Ladyfhip, that if fhe will neither

over-rate

over-rate the Captain's merit, nor undervalue
mine, and will put up with us both as we are,
and take all we have to offer in good part, i
will let the Captain and her Ladyſhip
fight their own battles, and ſettle their
private tiffs amongſt themſelves; but if ſhe
lets his violent temper diſturb my peace,
i will aſſert the rights of a huſband, and
deſire the Captain to keep his diſtance. But
be ſpeedy if you pleaſe, for he has left her two
days, and 'tis time ſomething ſhould be done.
And ſo believe me,

Dear Sir,

Your's every inch of me,

P. Le Neufieme.

P. S, On ſecond thoughts, ſoften that part where i
talk of keeping the tall Captain at a diſtance, for that's
a trick they are apt to ſerve me, when he, and my wife
and i go out together, and they will laugh as they once
did, when i was walking after them with all my might
in the Park, and a wag called out, " Well done little
one."

N U M-

N U M B E R VI.

T HAT the Happiness of life consists rather in Expectation than Enjoyment,
has been so frequently advanced, and so ably
supported by writers of former ages, and so
often repeated by those of our own times, that
it should seem impossible to urge any thing
new on so trite a subject : yet, perhaps the
elucidation of a well known fact, may produce Variety, where novelty ought not to be
expected ; particularly if the examples be ad-
dressed to those who may never before have
seen the object placed in a light adapted to
their pursuits.

THE Man of Business has little leisure to
peruse the speculations of Essayists ; and, if
he had, no arguments would prove suffi-
cient to convince him, that when he shall
have attained the object for which he daily
toils, he will at length find Happiness elude
his

his embrace, and often at the moment, when he fancies he has reached her. Such a man will tell you of the joy which reſt from un-remitting labour will afford; he will talk of the fatigue of buſineſs, anxious days, and ſleepleſs nights; and he will think it mad-neſs to ſuppoſe, that ſome years hence, (when he ſhall have acquired the fortune that his hopes have promiſed) he ſhall not enjoy Hap-pineſs which ſeems ſo intimately combined with affluence and eaſe. I will allow, that the profpeᴆ of this diſtant Hope is ſufficient to excite his utmoſt induſtry to poſſeſs the promiſed good; but let him beware how he quits that Induſtry, when he thinks he has no longer need of it; let him refleᴆ, that life without employment, can never bring him Happineſs. No human being, however ex-alted may be his rank and fortune, however enlarged and cultivated his underſtanding, can long be happy, without ſome objeᴆ of purſuit. Life is a ladder on which we climb from hope to hope, and by expeᴆation ſtrive to aſcend to enjoyment; but he is miſerable indeed, who fancies he has reached his higheſt hope, or who enjoys the utmoſt of his wiſhes; for thoſe who have been the moſt ſucceſsful in their refpeᴆive undertakings, have given

the

the gloomieſt deſcription of the emptineſs of human pleaſures.   The purſuit alone can yield true happineſs.; and, I affirm, that the moſt trifling object that has power to faſcinate the hopes of man, is worthy his attention. The money-getting Trader, looks with aſtoniſhment at the man of fortune, who neglects the palace of his anceſtors, to viſit foreign nations, without thoſe views which induce the merchant to correſpond with diſtant countries; and thinks, that were he but poſſeſſed of ſuch a family eſtate, England alone would ſatisfy his range of Happineſs; but when we talk of what would make us happy, we always talk of what is *not* in our poſſeſſion; and though mankind will ſometimes boaſt of ſatisfaction, which they know they do not feel; yet it is on the proſpect of ſome future good, that they truly dwell with rapture.

Though the Man of Buſineſs may not allow the truth of what I have aſſerted, the Scholar and Philoſopher will ſay it is a fact ſo evident, and ſo well eſtabliſhed, that it is almoſt as abſurd to go about to prove it, as it would be, to demonſtrate that the Sun gives light and heat: yet there is a middle claſs betwixt the buſy and the ſtudious, betwixt the man who ſpeculates with thought too

too much, and him who never thinks but to
get money ; I mean the leisure country
gentleman, who hunts, or shoots, or fishes,
as the seasons or the weather tempt ; and who
reads sometimes, because he can do nothing
else for his amusement. To him I shall address the remainder of this paper : for *he only*
can judge how truly I describe his feelings.

In a warm summer's evening, look at the
patient angler, his eye intently fixed upon a
floating quill ; a little guft of wind deceives
his fight, or his hand shakes the line and
causes an undulating motion of the cork ; his
heart bounds with transitory joy ; but all
is still again, and expectation gives a joy
more calm ; many minutes now elapse in
silent watchfulness ; at length his patience is
no longer kept in suspence, the float with frequent jerks is snatched below the surface of
the flood ; he feels the tremulous motion
in his hand, and pleasure thrills through all
his frame ; Anxiety and Hope, but not un-
mixed with Fear, engrofs his whole attention,
and cautiously he drags the struggling victim
to the light ; here when he views the unexpected magnitude of his glittering prize,
his joy is at its utmost reach ; what object
could at this moment tempt him to quit his
ftation ?

ftation ? Intent upon his fport, he one moment pulls, then feems to yield, then gently draws the exhaufted victim, till at length, exulting, he takes the fcaly prifoner in his hand : but alas ! with his victory his pleafure ceafes; for having difentangled the poor creature from his hook, he throws it down with indifference and proceeds to fifh again, that he may again enjoy the pleafure of anxious Expectation.

It is with peculiar propriety that I confider the Happinefs of the fportfman, fince I write this from my friend Aimwell's feat in B—fhire, where the feafon of the year and the neceffity of exercife, with a love of conformity, have led me to partake in the delights and fatigues of fhooting; and as I am not every day fo employed, I could not help attending to my fenfations during a walk of many hours and miles this morning; thefe I fhall endeavour minutely to defcribe.

We rofe and breakfafted an hour or two before our ufual time, that we might find our game at feed upon the ftubbles; a cloudy morning, with a brifk wind that dried the dew and gave the dogs every advantage of the fcent, communicated cheerfulnefs and vigour to our undertaking : hardly have we mounted

the

the firſt ſtile and ſtepped into the barley ſtubble, but Tohod old Sancho ſtands, Fop
backs him ſtaunchly, before *Hope* can fully
ripen into *Joy*, young Carlo daſhes in, and
the whole covey flies into a diſtant field of new
cut clover, and there we mark down every
bird; here is no time for diſappointment,
young Carlo is ſecured, and taken into couples
by the ſervant, and we ſtep forward with
eager ſtrides to the object of our hopes; after
walking briſkly down the hill, and having
toiled acroſs the valley, juſt as we reach the
corner of the field, panting with certainty of
falling on our prey, the birds with one
conſent mount into the air only a few yards
diſtance out of gun ſhot, and return into the
hedge of the ſame ſtubble field from whence
they were originally driven. Now, Hope
ſuggeſts, that being in the cover of the hedge,
the partridges will riſe one at a time and
yield us glorious ſport! full of this idea
we return with redoubled ardour the ſame
way by which we came, and though we now
aſcend at every ſtep, the way ſeems ſhorter
in proportion to our proſpect of ſucceſs. At
length, behold us on oppoſite ſides the hedge
in which we know our game is lodged, Sancho is on 'em! Fop winds 'em too! and
now!

now! with that palpitation, which only a
keen ſportſman can comprehend, we gently
beat the buſh; and forth from either ſide,
part of the covey ruſhes. My friend (who
ſeldom miſſes a fair ſhot) kills his bird. But
I, whether from too much eagerneſs, or too
little practice, ſhoot behind my mark; and
plainly diſcover, the moment I have fired,
why I have not ſucceeded; but there is no
time for recollection, much leſs for diſappointment; for there are more birds left.
Sancho is ſtiffened at the hedge, a few yards
diſtant. *In extreme haſte* my gun is charged
again, and I move on with pleaſing trepida-
tion: the partridge whirrs from the pointer's
noſe, and I take more certain aim; but
drawing the trigger, I diſcover, that in my
haſte I had forgot to prime. Now with my
eyes only I purſue the happy fugitive; and
this ſo occupies my thoughts, that diſappointment cannot find admittance; beſides, I exult in the reflection, that had my piece gone
off I ſhould moſt certainly have killed my
bird; and, while I am engaged in exultation,
and in priming the remainder of the covey
takes wing, and points the direction we muſt
follow. We now proceed, beating each field
with unrelaxing diligence: we try ſwathe
oats,

oats, or wheat, or barley stubbles; then look
the clover; or turnips are more likely: in
short each piece of land we enter, gives fresh
hopes: we are sure they must be there; but
having beat this field and that, in vain, we
have better founded hope of finding in the
next adjoining; nor does expectation droop,
beneath repeated disappointment; at length
the dogs *are certain* in the turnips, and
we approach with ardour, heightened by
delay; 'tis now a sportsman only can relish
what I feel; the dogs stand immoveable as
blocks of stone, and the heart beats with rapture at the approaching moment; while I
cautiously examine whether I *have primed
or not.*—At length a partridge rises with
rustling noise, and spreads his wings; my
well-aimed gun quickly stops him in his
flight and kills him on the spot.—This is the
moment which a novice in the field would
think the highest pitch of joy; but he is mistaken; the pleasure ceases with the victory;
the lifeless animal is negligently thrown into
the bag, and all the eagerness of hasty charg-
ing is repeated lest other birds should rise,
while I am unprepared. Thus the Happiness
of sporting, like that of every other object,
is more in expectation than enjoyment; and

having

having confined my illuſtration to the country,
gentlemen or ſportſmen, let none whoever
drew a trigger at a partridge, preſume to
judge of extacies which they may think over-
rated ; but let them remember that *energy*
even in trifles, is neceſſary to conſtitute felicity in active minds ; and that he who ſeeks
Happineſs with indifference in any purſuit of
life, will never find it ; he muſt be in earneſt,
whatever he undertakes ; and " what he
" does, he muſt do heartily."

N U M B E R VII.

NO fubject has, perhaps, more engaged
the attention of all ages and all countries, nor any in which there has been fo great
a difference of fentiment, as that of Education;
and when we reflect that it is a fubject
in which every individual is neceffarily inter-
efted, we fhall not wonder at the variety of
opinions concerning it; for every individual
who thinks at all, claims a right of thinking
for himfelf how to educate his own children,
or his own dependents. Unfortunately for
the peace of fociety, there are too many, who,
not fatisfied with this right in private,
prefume to intrude their fyftem of Education
on all around them.   Thus, in politics, in
religion, in the more abftrufe fciences, or in
the politer arts, we fee dictators and advifers'
laying down general rules for the obfervance
of all mankind.   But when a general plan is
propofed which affects a whole nation, we
fhould be cautious left fpecious promifes

D   of

of imaginary advantage, allure us beyond the bounds of prudence; fuch is the cafe with regard to a recent experiment, where piety and benevolence are held forth as the foundation, and an improved fyftem of morality reprefented as the fuperftructure: feduced by the hope of enlarging the underftanding, and increafing the happinefs of the rifing generation, all ranks commend a defign which they never examine, and applaud an inftitution, of which the future confequences have never been confidered; fuch is the phrenzy of expectation that has fuddenly feized all parts of this kingdom on the propofal for *Sunday Schools.* A plan originally fuggefted by fome perfons with good intentions, but in many places, I fear, moft ardently recommended from motives of Vanity in individuals, and a defire of becoming confpicuous in a popular meafure.

However impolitic it may be, to take the oppofite fide in fuch a queftion, I fhall endeavour to convince fome of my readers, that the *evils* to be dreaded from the plan, may greatly exceed the fuppofed *advantages.* But firft, obferve, I allow fo much of this plan to be *very good,* as tends to promote a regular attendance and decent behaviour of the poor, at fome place

of

of religious worſhip every Sunday. And now
I will proceed to the other boaſted advantages
of Sunday Schools. We are told that by dif-
fuſing the knowledge of *reading*, we ſhall enlarge the minds of the vulgar; I grant it;
but does it neceſſarily follow, that the lower
claſſes will become more *induſtrious*, more *virtuous*, or even more *happy?* Certainly not;
for were this the caſe, we might expect to find
thoſe qualities commenſurate to the proportion of knowledge in each individual, and
every day's experience teaches, that LEARN-
ING cannot ſecure its poſſeſſors from *indolence*,
from *vice*, and much leſs from *miſery.* So
far from it, I will boldly pronounce, that
it tends to promote the firſt, to conceal rather
than eradicate the ſecond, and to heighten
the poignancy of the latter.

A THOUSAND inſtances could be adduced to
prove this aſſertion, but I will confine myſelf
to one, as the moſt recently conſpicuous; and
illuſtrate my opinion by referring to the many
well authenticated accounts of the life and
character of that learned and pious prodigy
the late Dr. SAMUEL JOHNSON, whoſe ca-
pacious underſtanding and retentive memory,
made him a Coloſſus in literature, and a
Giant in precepts of true morality. Let us

ſee

fee how *Learning* defended this excellent man.
from thofe three great evils againft which
it is fuppofed to be a fpecific.   His *indolence*
he conftantly regrets, and his *induft·y* was the
effect of bitter want, which· not even all
his efforts were at times fufficient to remove;
he confeffes that he was never excited to labour but by neceffity, and would never allow
or believe that any other motive could ftimulate
a man to write or work; this cannot be called
induftry from a fenfe of duty, but hard labour
to avoid ftarving: and with Johnfon's fenfibility, fuch neceffary exertions of his mental
faculties were infinitely more painful than
the fevereft labour of the hufbandman or
mechanic.

Of the *virtues* or *vices* of this great man we
are not perfectly able to judge; for who can
dive into the heart of man to develope the
fecret motions of his mind? yet one obfervation on this good man's conduct is very
obvious, viz. We are at a lofs to reconcile
his inordinate fear of death, with his profeffed
belief of immortality; but that he either had
fecret vices which his prudence concealed, or
that his learning taught him to confider
as fuch, many occurrences of his life, about

which

which a lefs enlightened mind would have had no fcruples.

WITH refpect to his *happinefs* or *mifery*, the moft fuperficial obferver of his character will difcover, that he too feverely felt the prevalence of the latter, and that daily experience confirmed his favourite opinion; " that " the evils of human life over-balanced the " enjoyments of it ;" the horrors of death or infanity, were ever before his eyes ; and thus did the *moft learned* man of the prefent age, live in conftant wretchednefs from the anticipation of two evils ; one of which was inevitable and common to all, whilft the other never happened, and with a mind lefs enlightened would never have obtruded itfelf on his imagination.   It may be objected by fome, that I have chofen as an example, the character of one, who, though eminent in his learning, was fingular in his habits; but what human being is without fome peculiarity ? And his greateft proceeded from an excefs of what fome will call pious faith, and others enthufiaftic credulity.   This confideration naturally leads me to the fecond great advantage promifed by Sunday Schools, viz. That the knowledge of *reading*, will enable the poor to confult thofe books which contain the precepts of their duty in this life, and the hope of eternal happiness in a life to come. But who will deny that the labouring poor, may not be infinitely better inſtructed in all that it behoves them to know, by the arguments of their ſpiritual teachers, than they can collect themſelves from the voluminous books of Holy Writ, which having been compoſed at various times and for various purpoſes, frequently contain matter ſo myſterious, and doctrines ſo contradictory, that it has required the induſtry of the ableſt men to clear them from obſcurity, and extract that perfect ſyſtem of moral conduct, which the Chriſtian Religion (well underſtood) ſo admirably inculcates.

AMIDST the endleſs Variety of religious ſects, all are warranted by paſſages from ſcripture; yet there are many ſubverſive of all morality, and injurious to the well-being of ſociety. Such are the doctrines of Methodiſts ſo univerſally prevalent reſpecting the efficacy of faith, and ſaving grace. We ſee the country over-run by a ſet of people whoſe influence is prodigious, and daily increaſing. Some thouſand Preachers are diſſeminated through all parts of Eng-, land, and even planted in our moſt diſtant

territories,

territories, to plunder the fcanty pittance of credulous induſtry, while they recommend enthuſiaſm, and palliate vice.   There is no doctrine fo abfurd but texts may be found in fupport of it, by mutilating verſes, and joining difcordant parts; by interpreting figurative expreſſions literally, or making plain language bear a myſtic ſignification; and what man whoſe daily neceſſities require all his time, can find leiſure to collect or comprehend the whole extent and deſign of the facred writings?

WE know that the Preachers amongſt Methodiſts are of the loweſt claſs of the people, whom a little learning has made mad or cunning, and who prefer the indolent labour of their heads, to the more irkſome employment of their hands; but how will the number of theſe be increaſed when all can *read*, and when all claim the right of putting their own conſtruction on *what they read?* The minds of the poor will be enlightened indeed, but it will be with that *new light* which a witty Author obferves, " never " ſhines in upon the brain, but through " a *crack* of the fcull."   In the mean while, the duties of the prefent life will be all forgotten midſt the unneceſſary folicitude about the

life to come, which they are taught to confider will not depend on their conduct in this
world, but in growing grace and experience
of holy breathings, and all the cant terms
of myftical jargon. Having confidered the
promifed advantages of this fafhionable but
fuperficial plan for mending fociety, I fhall in
a future paper, fhew more at large, the evils
to be dreaded from its becoming general, and
anfwer the objections which its advocates
may be fuppofed to advance.

N U M B E R VIII.

In Continuation.

HAVING in a former paper expofed the fallacious promifes of advantage from SUNDAY SCHOOLS, I fhall now confider the probable mifchiefs which may accrue to the community, fhould the plan be univerfally adopted. There is no period recorded in the annals of hiftory, in which all mankind were perfectly equal ; nor is it poffible to imagine a ftate of Society, without certain degrees of fuperiority and fubordination amongft the in-dividuals of which it is compofed. We may compare fociety to a fluid, in which various particles are mixed, fome heavier, and fome lighter than others ; if the fluid be at reft, thefe will afcend, while thofe fubfide, till each particle of matter has found the due fituation in the general mafs allotted to it, by the laws of gravitation ; in like manner,

D 5

the

the individuals of fociety being different from each other, whether in property, in virtue, in genius, or in application, there will neceffarily follow an arrangement of them into higher and lower ranks of people ; there muft be mafters and fervants, rulers and labourers, patricians and plebeians, nor would a republic be lefs a ftate of abfurdity and confufion, whether it were deficient in legiflators and magiftrates, or in " hewers of wood " and drawers of water." The working poor are by far the moft numerous clafs, and when kept in due fubordination they compofe the riches of a nation ; but I contend that fome degree of ignorance is neceffary to keep them fubordinate, and to make them either ufeful to others, or happy in themfelves. What plowman who could read the renowned Hiftory of Jack Hickerthrift, or the ftory of the Seven Wife Men of Greece, would be content to whiftle up one furrow, and down another, from the morning dawn to the fetting of the fun ?—There is a fpirit of emulation in the meaneft kind, which urges him to excel his fellow-fervants. The latent fpark of ambition and thirft of praife, glows in every human breaft ; at prefent the contention of the clown is confined to the labour

of

of his hands : but as his mind becomes enlightened, he will defpife all fuperiority that
is merely manual ; he will neglect his daily
toil to indulge the fweet hope of future emi-
nence, and to promote that progrefs in the
improvement of his mind, which he flatters
himfelf is the road to eafe and enjoyment.
From an induftrious mechanic, or unwearied
hufbandman, he will afpire to be a keeper of
accounts, or even an expounder of the gofpel.
That the inordinate increafe and general dif-
femination of learning tend to extirpate induftry, is proved by the experience of nations and
individuals. A geographical author of repu-
tation obferves, that the people of Scotland
were greatly more induftrious before literature became fo univerfal ; and in England it
is a common obfervation among farmers,
that a hufbandman who can read and write,
is an incumbrance to a parifh ; and that
generally fpeaking, the parifh clerk is the
idleft perfon in the village.

I shall adduce another fact to fupport my
argument, though I am aware my humanity
will be arraigned for taking it from our Weft
India Iflands. The miferable flaves employed
in the plantations are human beings, with
minds little more inftructed than the mere

D 6   brute

brute creation; yet they perform labours for which human beings are absolutely neceffary, and for which no other animal could be fubftituted. It is obferved, not only by their too-commonly unfeeling mafters, but even by men of education and feeling who are refident in the country, that every enlargement of their underftandings, tends to leffen their habits of induftry, and to render more painful that fatigue, which ignorance alone enables them to fupport with chearfulnefs: I would not be underftood to recomend flavery, but to enforce the neceffity of keeping diftinct the feveral claffes of fociety. It is by too eagerly defiring to confound all degrees of rank, that men fo often render themfelves ridiculous, and their families miferable; each endeavouring to move in that fphere which is next above his own:—Thus the peer affumes the ftate and retinue of a monarch; the baronet betrays his country to become a peer; the indigent efquire pines to be made a baronet; the merchant quits his ufeful employment to be dub'd efquire; the fhopkeeper defpifes retail trade and calls himfelf a merchant; and every labourer who can read, will afpire to be a fhopkeeper: but where fhall we find

any

any to fupply the place of labourers? The clafs will be extinct. Not to be learned, will be a difgrace to humanity; and a learned labourer is a folecifm in language.

THREE objections will yet be made. *Firſt*, that nothing farther is intended than to teach the poor to *read*. *Secondly*, that this will enable them to pafs their leifure to advantage, in the perufal of good books; and *Thirdly*, that it is cruel to deny any rational creature, this fcanty pittance of mental acquirements. To the *firſt* I anfwer, that thofe who have been taught to *read* will teach themfelves to *write*, witnefs the walls of all our ftreets, and the obfcenity which fhocks the ftranger's eye. To the *fecond* I anfwer, that having learned to read, they will find bad books full as entertaining to pafs their hours away as good ones; and as to the *third* objection, that it is cruel to deny the poor an opportunity of reading any books, it is equally cruel to deny them the ufe of wine, of filk ftockings, or any other comfort which oppulence exclufively enjoys; for while the poor have wholefome food, warm cloathing, and good inftruction from their teachers, they have all the bleffings which their fore-fathers required, and with which

they

they were contented in their ſtation. The melancholy depravity in the morals of our poor, muſt be attributed to a very different ſource than that of ignorance: they are already too much enlightened. On a future occaſion I may point out more probable cauſes of the diſſolutenefs in the manners of the people, but this would now lead me too far from my ſubjeƈt. I ſhall therefore conclude with an appeal to thoſe who have experienced the benefits of a liberal education, whether they could with chearfulnefs ſubmit to the toils of any drudgery, which requires no exerciſe of the intelleƈtual faculties? Let me aſk the bankrupt merchant, if he could become a coal-heaver without murmuring? Or let the unbeneficed clergyman tell me whether he could follow the plow with hilarity? Rather would not each to fearn his daily bread, endeavour to procure employment, by which his mental acquirements might ſave him from the horrors of working with his hands?

THEN why ſhould we ſtrive to diſqualify a uſeful ſet of men, from purſuing thoſe inferior taſks which are performed with ignorant contentment. Reading is the ſolace of ſedentary leiſure; the beſt reſource of eaſe

and

retirement; but what have the bufy, the indigent, or the laborious to do with *that*, which neither time can allow, nor inclination ought to encourage?

THERE remains only one more objection. —" Who knows what mighty genius may " be loft by the want of a little cultivation?" Or to exprefs it more elegantly, I will put it in the words of Gray's Elegy.

Perhaps in this neglected fpot is laid,
   Some heart once pregnant with celeftial fire;
Hands, that the rod of empire might have fwayed,
   Or wak'd to extacy the living lyre.

But knowledge to their eyes her ample page,
   Rich with the fpoils of time did ne'r unroll;
Chill penury repreffed their noble rage,
   And froze the genial current of the foul.

To lament this fort of ftill-born genius, is like regretting the lofs of chickens that were never hatched; and though I may allow the lofs of a *poet in embryo* to be a great calamity to the country, yet with regard to *ftatefmen* and *prime minifters*, as there is feldom room for more than half a dozen of them to exer-cife their calling at the fame time, we may perhaps be able to fupply the neceffary quantity

tity from both Houſes of Parliament and the two Univerſities, till ſuch time as Sunday Schools ſhall have ripened the genius of the inferior claſſes in ſociety, by ſpoiling many millions of induſtrious labourers, in hopes of producing one " Village Hampden."

N U M B E R IX.

***

To 'Squire WEATHERCOCK.

S I R,

I AM one of the lads belonging to a Sunday School, and can't bear to fee fuch a good defign pull'd to pieces by you, or any body; we have boys amongft us, that will one day be judges, and bifhops, as Dr. Vainly often tells us; for, inftead of playing at trapball and cricket, and fuch like ungodly games, we are always employing our fpare time in gofpel difputations, and pofing one another with holy queftions: aye, and we have fome that would fet the doctor himfelf as faft as a church; and fo we have agreed to fend you fome to fhew how we get on; perhaps you may help us out with fome of the cramp enquiries; fuch as, Who was Adam's grandmother? Was the deluge frefh water or falt? Was the pidgeon fent from the ark, a cropper,

per, or a tumbler ? What was the name of Potiphar's wife ? And who was the father of the children of Zebedee ? All thefe myfteries have caufed warm and learned debates in our fchool ; but there is one that puzzles us more than all the reft ; and I fhall therefore give you the arguments made ufe of by the feveral difputants, that you may have fair play in anfwering it. The queftion is this : what is the right meaning of the word SUN-DAY, and how fhould it be fpelt. *Tom Vice* the blackfmith's fon, fays it fhould be SIN-DAY ; either becaufe it is the day when folks pretend repentance for the fins of the whole week, that they may go off afrefh ; or elfe, becaufe his father is more finfull that day than all the other fix put together ; for he regularly gets drunk every Sunday after evening fervice, and beats his wife and family for want of fomething to do. *Simon*, the fon of the Widow *Method*, who goes to the tabernacle, fays, that it fhould be fpelt SOME-DAY ; becaufe 'tis proper there fhould be fomeday in the week different from the reft. But little *Bob Amen*, the clerk's fon, is fure it fhould be fpelt SUMDAY, for two reafons ; firft, becaufe his father fettles half the books of the tradefmen in town ; and he has often

told

told him, that 'tis the only day, when people in bufinefs can find time to *fum* up all their accounts.   And Secondly, becaufe let the poor people earn ever fo much money in the week, the whole *fum* is often fpent at the ale-houfe in that one afternoon. I'm fure poor *Bob*'s father makes it his weekly practice, for the boy is the raggedeft in the whole parifh; but his father is a fad idle fellow, and never touches the fhuttle if he can get a penny by his quill.

THERE are various other conjectures about fpelling the word, and arguments in favour of SONDAY, and SOONDAY, and ZONDAY; but as they were lefs to the pur-pofe, I fhall only trouble you with my opi-nion, viz. that it is right fpelt in the com-mon way, SUNDAY; not as fome tell us, be-caufe Chriftians formerly worfhipped the fun on that day; for that, can never have been. The poor were never fo ignorant as to wor-fhip the Sun and Moon. No! though they had no *Sunday Schools* formerly, yet they had always preachers to tell 'em what was what; but fome folks fancy, when a man can't read, that he does not know the moon from a pew-ter plate, or the fun from a cotton fix. Now I take it that 'tis call'd SUNDAY; becaufe the fun fhines oftener on Sundays than on

any

any other day in the week ; at leaſt, if you will believe the farmers ; for when their hay or corn harveſt is about in fickle weather, they grumble ſorely every Saturday night, to think they muſt let it lie till a rainy Monday. Pray, Sir, tell me which of us is right ; for though I am the forwardeſt boy in the whole kit, I may be wrong in ſpelling a word some-times ; and ſo pleaſe to excuſe bad ſpelling, and truſt me, I will never be any thing elſe, but

S I R,

Your ſervant to command,

TIMOTHY TAKE-IT-A-PACE.

P. S. There is no caſhion to ſkuze bad ſpelling, for the Docter's Huſſikeeper, Madam Wheedle, has dun the job for me ; and I beant ſure ſhe deant'dd as mutch for the Docter when he puſhbliſt his laſt Sarmon pon Sunday Scools, for ſhe's a mortal cleaver of a woman, and got all her know when ſhe was very yung mung the charity boys.

MY

MY friend Timothy's ludicrous letter shall have a serious answer, nor let any one be offended at the contrast when he reflects that I profess *Variety*. Doubtless there will be some well disposed persons, to whom I shall give more offence by the *matter*, than the *manner* of this disquisition; but to such I shall only apologize, by telling them, that, amidst a Variety of opinions, truth may be discovered.   The Sunday, or more properly, the Sabbath, is an institution coeval with the creation itself, and sanctified by an express commandment in the decalogue, *as a day of rest from all labour*. No people professing any religion have hesitated to obey this injunction, founded on the truest policy, and originating in particular benevolence; although various have been the opinions respecting the manner in which it should be distinguished from the rest, and many differ in the day of the week in which it ought to be celebrated. The *Turks* hold the Sabbath on Friday, the *Jews* and one sect of *Christians* on Saturday, and the generality of Christians on Sunday.   But all agree in considering it as a day of relaxation from the labours of the week; and this respite from toil is not only extended to man, but to

all

all the animals which his ingenuity has rendered subservient to him. The SUPREME LAWGIVER foreseeing that without such repose, neither man nor beast could long endure the fatigue of constant exertion. The command for the observance of this day is expressed in the most unequivocal terms, " THOU SHALT DO NO MANNER OF WORK," to which Puritans have added, " *nor play nei-* " *ther.*" I cannot but smile at the absurdity of these pious Visionaries, who have converted the mandate of Benevolence, to the purposes of gloomy superstition. The *Sabbath* which in all other countries, is a day of festivity and harmless joy, is here become a scene of cheerless stupidity ; and the professors of a religion which teaches us to rejoice with them that rejoice, set one day in seven apart to look grave, to feel melancholy, and to go about sorrowing, that they may find occasion to weep with those that weep. This practice is by no means authorised by that of the primitive Christians, for they would not allow any symptom of humility to cloud the sunshine of that mirthful day; they even condemned the act of kneeling on the Sabbath, and prayers were said in all their congregations in a standing posture ; nay, during the

most

moſt rigorous obſervance of the faſts of Lent, the SUNDAY was conſidered as a day of *feaſt-ing*; the ſame opinions ſtill maintain their influence on the Continent, where Puritaniſm has not ſpread its narcotic poiſon ; all ſects of Chriſtians, whether Papiſts or Proteſtants, ſolemnize the day with feaſting and with mirth, with the ſound of the tabor and with merry dance and ſong ; ſuch, indeed, was the cuſtom of our anceſtors, " for James I. in " the year 1618, publicly declared to his " ſubjects, in what was called 𝕿𝖍𝖊 𝕭𝖔𝖔𝖐 " 𝖔𝖋 𝕾𝖕𝖔𝖗𝖙𝖘, theſe games following to be " lawful, viz. dancing, archery, leaping, " vaulting, may-games, whitſon-ales, and " morris-dances ; and did command that no " ſuch honeſt mirth and recreation ſhould be " forbidden to his ſubjects after evening " ſervice." This laudable permiſſion is ſtill accepted in ſome few parts of the kingdom ; where we ſee the village 'Squire calling forth the manly activity of his healthy neighbours to ſport upon his lawn, and make his fields alive with rural emulation ; in theſe diſtricts no man preſumes to bear his part in the amuſements of the day, who has not pre-viouſly recorded his appearance in the Tem-ple of his God ; for it is reaſonable that ſome

part

part of the Sabbath, should be dedicated in prayer and thankſgiving to the Lord of the Sabbath; but that the whole day ſhould be a ſeries of religious meditations and enthuſiaſtic fervor, could only be the conſequence of that miſconceiving zeal, which is a diſgrace to genuine Chriſtianity.

In a political view we experience its evil conſequences; all levity and diſſipation being baniſhed from the Sunday, our artificers to whom recreation is as neceſſary as reſt, make up this loſs by borrowing from the two adjoining days: thus St. Saturday and St. Monday, are moſt religiouſly obſerved in our large manufacturing towns. Inſtead, therefore of Sunday Schools, and evening lectures, let all ranks attend divine ſervice, at leaſt once in the day; and having done ſo, let the evening be rendered cheerful by publick demonſtrations of happineſs; not by that ſullen drunkenneſs which ſecret ſolace promotes. "Let the poor of each village fol- "low the jocund Rebeck, and join the "ſprightly dance:" then will they return to their labours with the Monday morning's dawn; and having finiſhed a ſix days taſk, will look forward to the Sunday as a day of reſt, and deliverance from all their cares.

NUM-

N U M B E R X.

———————————

THE univerſal deſire of appearing what
we are not, has been a common theme
with all writers; but while its prevalence
convinces us that it is in ſome meaſure natural to man, the variety of examples which
may hourly be adduced, will juſtify the repeated mention of ſo hackneyed a ſubjeſt.
We not only ſee people of all deſcriptions
ſtriving to impoſe on others, a belief of their
own riches, virtue, importance or underſtanding; but actually ſtruggling to appear happy
n the midſt of miſery, and cheerfully con-
ented with a lot, which they are for ever
viſhing and endeavouring to render leſs.
rkſome.

WHAT heightens the abſurdity of this
onduct, is, an attempt in ſome men to

impofe an appearance of happinefs from the poffeffion of qualities, which they really do not even *wifh to poffefs*. Such is the character of CHARLES EASY, who pretends never to be moved by the objects around him, who publicly defpifes the influence of the paffions, and ridicules the idea of feeling for another's concerns; he infinuates that to be anxious for what does not immediately relate to a man's own felf, is ridiculous and beneath the dignity of a rational being; but maintains that a man of moderate fortune, may pafs through life without trouble, and without anxiety, if he can acquire perfect indifference; and he is for ever labouring to convince his friends, that he poffeffes this quality in the higheft degree. I have many years been intimate with Charles, and a fhort acquaintance difcovered the contradictions of his life and profeffions; he has a heart to feel what his pride endeavours to difguife, and his honeft commiferation breaks forth in the midft of his counterfeit indifference; I have feen him fuddenly arife with an air of affumed infenfibility, at the recital of a tender tale, to hide the tear that gliftened in his eye. If the diftrefs of any human being is related in his prefence, he will coldly reply, that " people are apt to make

" the

" moft of fuch things;" but having artfully become informed of the fcene of wretchednefs, I have occafionally detected him in the act of vifiting and relieving the unfortunate fufferers, while he excufed his tendernefs by a carelefs avowal of mere curiofity; nor are his attentions confined to thofe of his own fpecies only, for I once faw him eagerly fpring forth to deliver a fly from the cruel gripe of a fpider; yet when I commended his generofity, he affured me that the only motive for his conduct, was the diffonant buzzing of the captive animal.   Thus does my friend pafs his life in contriving excufes, for being actuated by the brighteft ornament of human nature; and prides himfelf in a diffembled unconcernednefs, which he knows he fhould be miferable in really poffeffing.

On the contrary, old ALLSHEW is continually preaching up the charms of Benevolence, and afferts that all *happinefs* confifts in *good nature*, which he fays, includes every thing that is meant by the charity of Chriftian and the philanthropy of Heathen Philofophers; yet is this man a flave to envy, to refentment, and to fpleen, imperious in his family, cruel to his dependants, and quarrelfome to his acquaintance, continually la-

                menting

menting the infults of the world, and the malignity of others, and profeffing that *he* alone is happy, by the habit of putting favourable conftructions on premeditated affronts, and parrying infult by the guard of good nature; yet do his captioufnefs, his infolence, and his pride, expofe him to attacks, which his implacable refentment converts to never ceafing hatred.

Squire Big is confcious that he left the county in which his family had long refided, becaufe the neighbourhood refufed him that refpect, to which neither his rank, fortune, nor underftanding, had ever entitled him; yet is he continually boafting of influence which he dares not return to exert, and of importance which he never means to refume; folicitous to imprefs on others a fenfe of his own confequence, and to convince the world that he is fomebody when at home; while he is confuming with melancholy at his own infignificance, and only exifts to difguife the fatal truth that he is actually nobody any where.

Poor Ned Cramp is a good natured thoughtlefs fellow, who has fquandered away a fmall fortune, to make the world think he had a large one; he talks of money in the funds which he has long fold out, and

laments

laments the tardiness of tenants, whose rents he long since assigned to satisfy his creditors; he is constantly advising with his friends how to put out sums on the best security, while he is actually borrowing money at exorbitant interest; he talks of prudence and œconomy as " things well enough for people in narrow " circumstances," but thanks Heaven " he " has no need of such virtues to secure the " permanency of his happiness," nor is he induced to impose on others to support a false credit, or to indulge extravagance, but to gratify the vain desire of being thought a *monied man*. Thus does he waste his days in misery, that he may be deemed happy, and will end them in poverty, that he may be esteemed affluent.

DOCTOR D * * has but one topic in all companies; a few minutes conversation will bring round his favourite subject, and you soon discover, that implicit obedience in a wife, and the strictest subordination to her husband, constitute all his ideas of domestic happiness; his greatest glory seems to arise from the consciousness that he is absolute master in his own family: of this boasted superiority his friends can seldom bear witness, for he rarely invites them to his house. Hav-

ing

ing dined there lately, I perceived his reafon, for during the repaft, while he was conftantly engaged in afferting his authority, his wife was as anxious to difpute it, and the comforts of conviviality were banifhed by this domeftic contention, which gradually increafed till the Lady left the table. However, the Doctor triumphed in this victory, I could difcover that he dreaded fhe would return to the combat, and that the fufpenfion of hoftilities would end with my vifit.

There can be no fituation, however elevated, that will infure continual happinefs ; nor any fo abject as to be without enjoyment ; indeed happinefs and mifery feem fo neceffarily united, that they are equally difperfed through all ranks of fociety ; and though we cannot perfuade ourfelves we are content or happy, we wifh to conceal from others every appearance to the contrary ; we derive happinefs from being thought to poffefs it, and comfort ourfelves in wretchednefs if we can difguife it from others.

I shall conclude my examples of feeming contentment, with a letter from one, who can have little reafon to difguife the fenfe of his melancholy fituation : it is from a criminal under fentence of twelve months

confinement

confinement in a folitary cell of a county prifon ; he is without friends, without property, without character, and without any neceffary of life except the fcanty allowance which hard labour procures midft the horrors of a dungeon ; yet he wrote the following letter, and delivered it to the Keeper to be forwarded to a brother at a diftance.

" DEAR JACK,

" THIS comes with my kind love, hoping it will find you in good health and fpirits, as it leaves me at this prefent writing, thanks to nobody for it; I live in a pleafant part of the kingdom here, and only for the diftance between us not fo much amifs ; the people are not over and above fociable, and fo I never mixes with none of 'em ; work is in great plenty here, and provifions coft us nothing; the houfe I live in is newly built, and they fay 'tis one of the beft of the fort in all England, for they can make up better than forty feparate bed rooms every night. I was forry to hear poor Bob was catched-out laft Affizes ; but no matter for that, they fay Botany Bay is a rare country, and worth while to go on purpofe to fee, for 'tis quite another world.   And fo hoping we may all go there one time or other, this concludes me,

Dear Jack,

Your's till death,

Tom Filch."

P. S.   Direct to me, at A * * Bridewell, where I have fallen into a job of work, that will hold me beft part of next winter.

N U M-

NUMBER XI.

Mr. WEATHERCOCK.

SIR,

YOUR predeceffors have all attempted to fix a ftandard of *wit*, frequently attempting to confine, what feems uncontroulable, and to give definitions of what is indefineable, becaufe it is rather to be felt than defcribed; befides, *wit* is as much under the dominion of fafhion, as a cap or a petticoat, a phyfician or a bathing place; and what one century applauds, becomes vulgar, low, and defpicable in the next. The Spectator has in a feries of effays, laboured to fhew of what wit does *not* confift; but I have often confidered him as too fevere on one fpecies of wit, which is purely colloquial, and what is only

E 5

calculated

calculated for converfation, authors are apt
to confider with contempt ; without reflecting that though many can talk, few can
write, and there are degrees of excellence in
both. We may compare the feveral fpecies of
writing or talking with each other, in fomething like the following manner :

A Tragedy—to an interefting or melancholy
   fact well told.

A Comedy—to a laughable event related
   with humour.

A Hiftory or Voyage—to a long ftory of a
   man's felf, or his family.

A Satyr or Lampoon—to the fame thing, but
   told of other people.

An Elegy—to a lamentation, or occafional
   complaining.

A Sonnet— to a declaration of manly fentiments, or tender paffions.

A Sermon—to a curtain-lecture, that produces uneafy fleep.

And an Epigram—may be compared to a pun,
Yes Sir, a pun.   Now whether Mr.
WEATHERCOCK, you are a punfter or not,
as you profefs *Variety*, I expect you will
patiently hear my vindication of this very
antient, very ingenious, and very laughter-
caufing branch of the fcience of *chit-chat*,
                                    though

.though in direct oppofition to the mighty
Dean, who denounced " *God's judgment againft
punfters.*" ⋅ ⁊⋅   ⋅   ⋅

You fee.I have ranked the pun in converfation, with the epigram in compofition;
and to expect all the requifites of focial language from a punfter, would be as unreafonable, as to expect a comedy from an epi-
grammatift.   But there is this material difference betwixt a pun and an epigram, in
favour of the former; viz. that whether a
punn be very good, or very bad, it is allowed
to anfwer the end of its creation, by producing either furprize or laughter.   ⋅   .

⋅ .I can fee no reafon why in our own times
we should be fo faftidious about punning in
converfation, when we have the authority of
the higheft antiquity, as well as that of ages
immediately preceding our own, to fuppofe,
that the greateft and wifeft men, occafionally indulged in this derided exercife ; and
fince we find frequent fpecimens of puns in
the beft writers, both facred and prophane,
it is furely a very poor excufe to fay, that it
proceeded from a compliance with the de-
praved cuftoms of the times ; for if thofe
times were fufficiently correct, to afford examples of eloquence, wit, and humour,

         why

why should we be so squeamish as to refuse a place, to any species in the catalogue of wit? Our best dramatic authors abound with puns, because they describe the conversation of the times; nor was this kind of wit applicable to clowns only, for we find it in the mouths of kings and princes. *Hamlet* speaking of the king his uncle, who was become his mother's husband, and whose perfidy and hatred he suspected, calls him, " *a little more* " *than kin, but less than kind.*" Every school-boy is delighted with the ingenuity of the allusion to two words; one of four letters, and the other of three; by which *Hamlet* expresses, that the king was more than merely of *kin* or related, though not so much as possessing one *kind* affectionate regard; but before the boy can well comprehend the meaning, he is told it is an execrable pun.

HOMER makes ULYSSES call himself No-MAN, that when the Giant bewails the loss of his eye, it may appear accidental by his saying, that No man had put it out. HOMER and SHAKESPEARE are great authorities, and if their puns are not more frequent; much may be attributed to the nature of a pun, which like an extempore, loses its force by being written. But while modern criticks

ridicule

ridicule the use of punning, let them remember that the Pope holds his supremacy
over the Church of Rome, from an expreſſ-
ion in the 18th verse of the 16th chapter of
St. Matthew. "Tu es Petrus, et super
"hanc Petram ædificabo meam Ecleſiam."
Which the French render thus : "Tu es
"Pierre & sur cette Pierre, j'edifierai mon
"Egliſe." Where the alluſion to the two
words, *Peter* and a *rock*, would now be
called a pun ; for I muſt explain to the mere
Engliſh reader, that in moſt European languages, theſe two words are expreſſed by
sounds nearly ſimiliar, though it does not
hold in Engliſh ; and this gave occaſion to a
French bigot to declare, "that the Engliſh
"nation muſt have been predeſtinated here-
"tics, ſince their very language would not
"allow them to underſtand and acknow-
"ledge, the origin of that power which the
"Holy See aſſumes." If neither HOMER,
nor SHAKESPEARE, nor the Sacred Writings, can do away the obloquy caſt on punning by the SPECTATOR, I will prove that
one of thoſe few inſtances, in which he
departed from his uſual taciturnity was to
utter a PUN. Every admirer of that excellent Eſſayeſt, will recollect the anſwer made

by

.by him respecting a sign, in which Sir Roger
de Coverley's portrait had been changed to a
Saracen's head; when the Knight asking the
Spectator which it was most-like, he replied,
" much might be said on both sides.", Here
is manifestly a punning allusion to the two
sides of the projecting sign, as well as the
proposed question; for had the sign been
fastened flat against the wall of the house, as
signs are at present, the wit of the reply
would have been all on one side, and as a
punster would say, "very flat." I may also
refer the reader to No. 454, and a letter in
455, besides many other papers in the Spectator, for puns which afford delight. In the
Tatler, the account of the Staff and Ex-fam-
ilies are strings of puns. See No. 11, 35,
49, and 54, in the first vol. only,

 I do not pretend to vindicate punsters on
all occasions, but I wish to snatch them from
the contemptuous sneer of those dull dogs in
society, who being unable to raise a laugh
themselves, are envious at every attempt to
do so in another; or those keen witlings,
whose brilliancy of imagination, enables them
by an unexpected repartee, to turn the shafts
of ridicule on every object around them. No
species of wit can be at all times welcome;
the

the most inoffensive joke, becomes insult in the house of mourning; and a pun may be hardly tolerable in the moment of terror or calamity. Such was the case a few nights ago, when I was taking shelter with my friend QUIBBLE under a lime tree; the thunder rolled inceffantly tremendous, and while the vivid lightning illumined all the horizon; I obferved that there was fomething very *fublime* in the fcene around us: "liter-"ally *fublime*," faid he, "for we are ftand-"ing *under* a *lime* tree." I was more pleafed with my friend on another occafion: when we had a full hour been expofed to the dull metaphyficks of a profeffed deift, who wound up his argument by faying, "we may talk "of faith, and repeat a creed by rote like a "parrot; but anfwer me this: is it poffible "for reafon to believe incredibilities?" QUIBBLE anfwered, "I believe *in creed abili*-"*ties* to remove doubts, which reafon may "fuggeft, but can never fatisfy." The philofopher turned on his heel with contempt and mortification; obferving, it was in vain to argue with a punfter: while I rejoiced at any means of putting an end to fo tirefome an oration.

A WELL

'A **well** timed pun is often the source of merriment, as I before observed, whether it be very good, or very bad; and it is a species of wit much oftner used by good authors, than is at first imagined, or than some will allow; for a pun may be defined, *" the incongruous comparison, or combination of " similar sounds, conveying different ideas;"* such for instance, are often the fictitious proper names of feigned persons in all works of invention, and the dramatis personæ of a play, is frequently nothing more than a string of well-adapted puns.

Maskwell—is a villian in disguise.

Touchwood—is one easily kindled by the flame of love.

Careless—is a plain easy unaffected character.

Brisk—reminds us of the sudden effervescence of cyder or champaign.

Froth—is more like the permanent emptiness of a whip'd syllabub.

And Plyant—conveys the idea of extreme ductility.

Yet

Yet are all thefe words, which we have no re-
pugnance to admit as proper names of men
and women. Of the fame kind are the Spectator's CAPTAIN SENTRY, for an officer in the
army; and Sir ANDREW FREEPORT, for a
wealthy merchant.   In this more exalted
fpecies of punning, no man has been more
fuccefsful than the lively author of the *New
Bath Guide*; and I appeal to the readers of
that exquifite performance, whether the pleafure they received from its perufal, has not
been often heightened by the ludicrous allufions in the names of the characters defcribed.

HAVING faid fo much in favour of punning,
I will allow that a *mere punfter*, may be a nui-
fance to fociety.   By this, I mean *one* who is
for ever on the look out to entrap a poor fingle
inoffenfive word, and torture it into fome new
ftrange meaning; who never gives an anfwer
without a quibble; who confiders the *words*,
and not the *matter* of converfation; and who
feems liftening to an argument, while he is
only ringing changes on the words and fyl-
lables of which it is compofed.   Such a one,
though he may by chance excite merriment,
by blundering on fomething ludicrous, becomes tirefome by conftant efforts to furprize,

prize, and tedious by repeated failure.
While I condemn the *mere punster*, I will
not forget that I am the champion of punning
as an occasional source of *Variety*, surprize,
and cheerfulness in convivial meetings; but
the essence of a good or bad pun, consists in
its novelty, and the unexpected manner in
which it is produced. Who could have refrain-
ed from smiling, had he been present, when a
traveller accidentally met and asked another, if
he intended to "make any stay at Cambridge?"
to which he abruptly replied, "Sir! do you
" take me for a stay-maker?" Or who but
would have acknowledged ingenuity in the
boy, who excused a vulgar illiterate lad
for defacing a mile-stone, by saying, "that
" he had proved great proficiency in arith-
" metic, who could *so easily reduce figures by*
" *vulgar fractions.*"

I SHALL at once explain the origin of
my partiality for punning, when I inform
you that I belong to the Herald's Office;
where the mottos, and bearings, and names,
of great families, afford inexhaustible examples of this ancient science. If I find
you take notice of this, I may, perhaps,
at a leisure hour, look into our books
respecting

respecting your own name and family, and gratify you with a more ample account and genealogy, than private records can supply. And so

Dear Sir,

Yours,

PHILIP PHILOPUN.

NUM-

NUMBER XII.

THERE appears to be no *Vice* to which mankind is subject, but there is also some *Virtue*, which is exactly its reverse: thus, *Courage* is the opposite to *Cowardice*, *Modesty* to *Impudence*, *Humility* to *Pride*, and *Integrity* to *Deceitfulness*; but it does not always happen, that each Virtue is considered amiable in proportion as its opposite Vice is deemed detestable. Is it that Men love rather to condemn than praise? In other words, that to punish evil with reproach, is more congenial to our nature, than to reward the good with commendation? or, is the world in general, so good, that instances of vicious conduct being rare, we seize more eagerly the opportunities of censure, than applause? I am led to this train of thought by having frequently observed how different is the treat-

ment

ment of *Gratitude* and *Ingratitude*; the latter is juftly execrated as the blackeft vice that can difgrace the human breaft. "Ingrati-tude," fays *Shakefpeare*, "is as if this mouth "fhould tear this hand for feeding it;" yet its oppofite, Virtue, is feldom honoured with the "meed of praife;" and the moft ge-nerous fervice that a man may render to his benefactor, is damped by the cold and chill-ing remark, "that he has only done his "duty."

IF in all the occurrences of our refponfi-bility, we could enfure ourfelves this feem-ingly fcanty pittance of reward, we might pafs through life with fatisfaction, and meet even death without a fear; but while fo few can boaft that they have *done their duty*, it is invidious to withdraw our warm applaufe from thofe whofe conduct may deferve it. Great opportunities of exercifing Virtue, do not prefent themfelves every day; but our gratitude can never long remain inactive: there is hardly a moment of our lives, but may remind us of benefits received, and obli-gations due. The truly pious man, will ne-ver retire to reft, or wake from fleep, but with thankfgiving to that BEING, who dif-

penfes

penfes happinefs with life, and makes adverfity itfelf a fource of future bleffing.

INGRATITUDE is a conftant fubject of complaint with all mankind; and this, I fear, proceeds from their being more fenfible of the benefits conferred by them, than of thofe which they receive. If a man do a good office, he never forgets that he has done it, he never fees the perfon whom he has obliged, but with a felf congratulation of applaufe; on the contrary, if he receive an obligation from another, he may exprefs a fenfe of gratitude, at firft, with fervour perhaps unfeigned; but time fo moderates the ardour of this fenfe, that he at length forgets his benefactor, and even views him with indignation if he but difcontinues for a while his wonted favours. My friend *Aimwell* complained to me of the ungrateful treatment he fuffered from the tradefmen of the neighbouring market town. The grocer, who at firft bowed to the earth with gratitude, for the honour of rankingthe *'Squire* amongft his cuftomers; becaufe he occafionally fupplied the Hall with certain petty articles: now that he furnifhes almoft every thing, mutters to the fteward, becaufe the tea ufed in the family is bought elfewhere. And the butcher,

who

who fupplies the houfe with meat, claims the liberty of courfing, when he pleafes, in the park and fields adjoining; and though he owes his exiftence, as a tradefman, to the 'Squire, yet he refents (as publickly as he dares) the meffage of the Keeper, to remove his fports to greater diftance: forgetful of the conftant debt of gratitude, he confiders as an injury, the refufal of that priviledge, which he would not prefume to expect, but from a caufe that ought to make him the more grateful.

This fort of ingratitude is much more univerfal than we at firft imagine; for I confider as very nearly allied to it, every faftidious or unreafonable propenfity, whether relating to man or beaft, or even to inanimate objects, which leads us to expect *more*, becaufe *much* is already given: thus while we look on a well painted picture, if any little diftortion of a limb, or error in the drawing, be difcovered, we turn from it with difguft, regardlefs of the numerous excellencies with which it may otherwife abound.

Those who have moft to give, are moft likely to complain of man's ingratitude; for this reafon a king obferved, *that his power of difpenfing favours, was the moft painful tafk of royalty,*

royalty, since he never gave a place away, but he made ninety-nine discontented, and one ungrateful subject. Nearly to the same purpose, was my Lord B—'s answer, on being asked why he discontinued giving annual balls ? He said, " that his rooms were not large enough " to contain more than two hundred per- " sons ; and that he feared making all above " that number, who were his friends, his " enemies ; for he had observed, that those " ladies who were invited, forget it before " next year ; but those who were not invit- " ed, never forget it while they live."

I will conclude my observations on this subject, by describing the character of a clergyman, now actually living in the county of Norfolk; but whose real name I shall disguise under that of EUCHARIS. This gentleman was early in life presented to the adjoining Rectories of B * * * and B * *, by a patron, who at that time was unmarried ; and therefore had no idea of securing a reversion of the livings to a younger son ; and Eucharis has now enjoyed the benefice full thirty years. Being hospitable with œconomy, and charitable with prudence, the income of his living, with some private fortune, have enabled him to live in splendid afflu-

ence,

ence, and leave a faving every year for extraordinary purpofes, which gratitude has
pointed out.   He firft confidered the heavenly Mafter whom he ferves, as his original and
greateft patron ; and, though his piety would
check the prefumption of repaying for the
bleffings he enjoys; yet he knows, that every
attempt in man to fhew his gratitude, is acceptable in the fight of Heaven.   With this
view, he has confecrated part of the annual
favings of his income to repair an ancient
Gothic ftructure, where he exhorts his flock
to worfhip; and has actually expended many
hundred pounds to reftore and beautify the
temple of his God.   This fingular act of
piety was fecretly conducted, he raifed an
annual fum from his parifhioners, that he
might not be fufpected of the fact, and cele-
brates the rebuilding of the church, as the
effect of voluntary contribution ; nor did he
neglect any other duties of a Chriftian, to
fave the money fo appropriated ; for his private well directed charities, amount to nearly
half his income : his barns and ftore-houfes
are a repofitory for the induftrious poor, who
buy of him all the neceffaries of life, at a
price confiderably lefs than what he pays for
them : he never gives money to the idle, but

F

liberally

liberally recompenses labour, and relieves with tenderness, the wants of age, of sickness, and infirmity, demonstrating true gratitude to Heaven, by acts of charity to man.

He has shewn in a manner, almost unprecedented, his gratitude to his earthly patron: that gentleman died about ten years since, leaving an estate entailed on his eldest son, and three other boys so scantily provided for, that they could ill afford the expence of a learned education. Eucharis knew this, and taking them to the Parsonage, he considered them all as part of his own family; instructed them in the learned languages himself, and sent them to the University to qualify them for orders, that they might in time fill those benefices which are in the gift of their elder brother. Nay, he has done more, he has actually resigned one of those livings which he himself received from their father, to the eldest of these three, who is just become of age to hold it : having no nearer relations, he considers the descendants of his patron as his heirs ; and thus prolongs his gratitude to a second generation. A character so unexampled, will appear to many the produce of invention; but though I might offend the modesty of my friend, by

men-

mentioning his name, I have recorded the county, which actually poſſeſſes ſo bright an ornament of human nature; and my heart, feels (I truſt) a laudable degree of pride and exultation, when I reflect, that I am perſonally acquainted with this glorious pattern of unabating gratitude.

P. S. Since I wrote this Eſſay, I have been moſt deeply afflicted by the following paragraph in the Norfolk Chronicle, of 22d March, 1788. "On Monday laſt, died the "Rev. William Hewett, Rector of Bacons- "thorpe and Bodham."

NUMBER XIII.

THE various complaints of my numerous correspondents, would seem at first
sight to confirm an opinion which has often
prevailed, " that in the course of Human Life
" there is more *Misery* than *Happiness*." But
having never subscribed to this opinion myself, so I shall endeavour to convince my
readers that it is erroneous, and that if *Happiness* does not absolutely exceed *Misery* in the
world, yet at least the portion of each is
nearly equal.   Let us first consider by whom
this doctrine is chiefly advanced, and we shall
find it to be by those, who have communicated their discontented thoughts in *writing* to
the public ; for in *conversation*, few men wish
to represent themselves less happy than they
are.   It is, therefore, to the class of *Authors*,
that we must trace this melancholy observation; and I will allow that if any profession be

more

more miferable than another, it is that of
Authorfhip; from the poor drudge who
writes a paragraph in a garret, to that great,
and rich, and royal Author, who declared
that " *Increafe of Wifdom was increafe of Sor-*
" *row.*" For the man who has *time* and *abi-*
lities to write, has alfo time and abilities,
to think.

THE idle Speculatift, whether groan-
ing under the preffure of poverty, or gafp-
ing on the pinnacle of affluence, will occafionally be led to feel the emptinefs of all
human enjoyments, and complain with So-
LOMON, that " all is Vanity;" he will look
back on attempts in which he has failed with
vexation, and on thofe in which he has fuc-
ceeded with contempt, at their little worth;
he will look forward with chilling fear at future Hopes, and fhrink from Undertakings, accompanied with hazard. Yet amidft the difguft of retrofpection, and the gloom of hope-
lefs profpects, there will be always fomething
to folicit his prefent attention, fome trifling
engagement or fome frivolous avocation,
that may enable him at leaft to enjoy the prefent moment; and if he ferioufly reflect upon
his feelings, he will perceive that he is very
feldom indeed unhappy at what has happened
to him, but rather at the dread of what may

F 3   happen.

happen. The SPECTATOR has obſerved, that
" were a man's ſorrows and diſquietudes to be
" ſummed up at the end of his life, it would
" generally be found, that he had ſuffered
" more from the apprehenſions of ſuch evils
" as had never happened, than from thoſe
" evils that had really befallen him;" and
he adds, that " of thoſe evils which had real-
" ly befallen him, many have been more pain-
" ful in the proſpect, than by their actual
" preſſure." This obſervation holds good
through all the ſtages and conditions of life,
whether the evils be real or imaginary, whether they proceed from mental or corporeal
affections. I do not pretend to aſſert that
there is no evil in bodily pain, but whoever
has experienced much of it, muſt confeſs, that
it is never continual or unabating. The
Great Diſpenſer both of good and evil, has ſo
formed our bodies, that the moſt excruciating
agonies have moments of remiſſion, and the
pains of the gout, the ſtone, or of child birth,
are frequently relieved by natural intervals of
mitigation, without the aſſiſtance of Lauda-
num, which never fails to give temporary
eaſe from pain; and when the body is again
reſtored to health, and freed from torture, to
look back on paſt ſufferings is one of the
greateſt

greateſt ſources of human enjoyment: I am
acquainted with a gentleman, who amidſt ample poſſeſſions, having little to excite his hopes
or fears, is occaſionally apt to become liſtleſs
and diſſatisfied with life, till a ſevere fit
of the gout reminds him of his happineſs, an
ardent ſenſe of which he moſt gratefully
expreſſes at the termination of every pa-
roxyſm. Thus it is with the mind alſo; from
whatever ſource our miſery proceeds, it is never without alleviation, if we will admit it.

'Tɪs not the actual exiſtence of preſent
calamity, but the anticipation of its conſequences, that afflict and torture us. The
loſs of a friend preſents us with a view of ſo-
litude and privation of his future converſation, in which we might never have again
delighted. The loſs of a child puts a period
to hopes which might never have been rea-
lized, had the child ſurvived. The man to
whom conſtant occupation is not neceſſary to
ſupply his daily food, or to promote his ambitious views, will ſometimes be depreſſed by
the employment of his mental faculties; he
will look forward with dejection, to events
which may never happen, and ſhrink from future evils, which he may never have to
encounter: while the trifling buſtle and en-

F 4

gagements,

gagements, which belong to each fucceeding day, will intereſt his feelings, and afford him happineſs if he will fuffer himſelf to be diverted by them; but when he directs his thoughts to diſtant years, he fancies he ſhall be miſerable and loſe his reliſh for the joys he now poffeffes; he forgets that freſh objects (equally frivolous perhaps with thoſe that now engroſs him) will have their power to charm. The mind of man accommodates it-ſelf to every ſituation, and like one who at the firſt entrance into a hot houſe, feels a fuffocating heat, which gradually becomes only a comfortable warmth; ſo there is no change of life, no reverſe of fortune, and no loſs of friends or connections, that time and habit will not reconcile; we grieve now leſt we ſhould have cauſe to grieve hereafter, and are unhappy through fear of really becoming ſo; we ſee the approaching evil, but are blind to the obſtacles that may prevent its ever reaching us, and while we fix our eyes on the *Mountain of Calamity*, we forget that poſſibly our deſtined road may lie in the *Valley of Peace*, which ſurrounds its baſe: or that perhaps, we may ſink into the *River of Death*, which flows at its foot, and ſometimes kindly ſnatches us from the painful labour of ſtrug-

gling

gling with insuperable difficulties. After all, there is one *source* of consolation which should never be overlooked, viz. That we are often mistaken in our judgment of what is *good* or *evil*. Thus the Widow Hopeless, whose husband died insolvent, leaving her with six small children, in a state of dependance on the bounty of her friends, has lived to see those children each settled in the world in affluence, and has repaid her Benefactors the obligations she received.

There is, perhaps, no source of mental anxiety and pain, more common or more poignant than that of providing for a numerous offspring. What agony can equal that of an unsuccessfully industrious man, who by his failure, dreads the utter ruin of the fortune of his family? imagination paints his children beggars, and himself advanced in years no longer able to support them; but let him not despair, let him look round, and he will find in every district of the capital, and in every town in England, numerous families like that of Widow Hopeless, who have risen to affluence and power, from circumstances the most unpromising; at the same time that he will see the single heirs of

great

great paternal riches, reduced to sudden or
to gradual poverty. But who can affert that
affluence or power will actually fecure felicity to their poffeffors? Or that by entail-
ing *wealth* he can entail *happinefs* on his pofterity? Wealth too often is the caufe of leifure,
and he who is not employed will be moft
wretched; the man of bufinefs has the faireft
chance for happinefs; the fervant is oftener
happy than his mafter; and thofe who have
been nurfed in the enfeebling lap of indolence
and eafe, envy the lot of the poor labouring
hind; the felicity of fhepherds has been the
conftant theme of Poets; what idle man
does not envy the induftrious cottager, and
feel the force of an old fong, beginning
nearly in thefe words:

   " Strong LABOUR gets up at the firft
      " morning dawn,
   " And ftoutly fteps over the dew fpangled
      " Lawn;
   " For with him goes HEALTH from a cot-
      " tage of thatch,
   " Where never Phyfician had lifted the
      " latch."

CHILDREN frequently owe their misfor-
tunes to the too provident ambition of their
                      parents.

parents.   Thus becaufe our own times have given an example of two fons of a mere country Curate, having rifen to the higheft honors in the Law and Church, every fond father hopes to fee his fon a Bifhop or a Chancellor; rather let him fow and cherifh the feeds of humility, content, œconomy, and obedience to fuperiors, than plant the dangerous flifts of ambition, or graft on their tender minds, the hope of greatly augmenting riches; by fuch conduct he will render his children more ufeful members of fociety, and infinitely happier in themfelves. We are feduced by wifhes which we have no right to encourage, and are miferable at the failure of hopes built on bad foundations. Let us then rather enjoy our prefent happinefs, undifturbed by what may or may not befall us in a future diftant period, a fentiment fo well expreffed by Horace, that I cannot refift the temptation of quoting it as a conclufion :

" *Carpe diem, quam minimum credula poftero.*"

NUMBER XIV.

—————————————————

S I R,

YOUR paper, which has found its
way into Wiltſhire, affords a very acceptable amuſement to thoſe, who like myſelf,
have nothing to do, and have not reſolution or
perſeverance to follow one continued ſeries of
ſtudy, but delight to read without much
attention, and therefore, prefer that ſort of
Literature, which like " the juſtly famous
" Pill, may be taken without loſs of time,
" or hindrance of buſineſs ;" of this kind
are moſt periodical publications, and " tho'
" laſt not leaſt," in my eſteem, *Variety*; for
as to the daily Papers, they are rather the ve-
hicles of Politics than Literature, dealing
out *old* Anecdotes under the title of *News*.

I WAS particularly pleaſed with your elu-
cidating by rural ſports, that well known
maxim,

maxim, " that Happinefs confifts more in
" Expectation than in Enjoyment ;" and alfo
with your late paper on the *Anticipation
of evil*, fhewing, that we are often more miferable from the fear of what may happen, than
from the actual calamity under which we
groan ; of the latter I am myfelf an example.

ABOUT a month ago, in returning from a
fox chace on Nimrod, (who never before
made a ftumble in his life) a rolling ftone
threw him down, and I falling with my right
leg under him, fo bruifed my knee, that
I have never fince been able to fet my foot to
the ground ; when the accident firft happened I was dejected beyond meafure, not fo much
from the actual pain I fuffered, as from the
horrors of being confined many weeks during
the beft feafon for hunting : the firft week
after my fall I flept but little, partly from the
fever attending the contufion, but more
from my uneafinefs under confinement,
(having never before known the misfortune
of two days illnefs) I am now almoft free
from pain, but the limb is fo weak, that I am
ftill confined, and have had for the laft fort-
night paft, full leifure to reflect on my various fenfations during my imprifonment.

You

You can hardly conceive, Sir, the prodigious
revolution which has taken place in my
mind. Many things now delight, which
formerly afforded no satisfaction, and I look
with indifference on pursuits, which before
appeared to me the most engaging. I long to
get out, not because I wish to hunt, (for I
care little whether I ever hunt again,)
but methinks, I should enjoy walking round
my garden, to give directions to my people.

There is a very sensible and learned
Clergyman in the parish, of whose company I
have seldom been solicitous, because he is no
fox hunter, and takes little satisfaction in the
conversation of those, whom my favourite sport
used to bring to my table; for these reasons,
I have never till now, had leisure to consider
his good qualities; indeed, I had the less inclination to cultivate his acquaintance, from
an observation he made the first time we met:
he said, that "although occasional fox hunt-
"ing might be a rational amusement to those
"who required strong exercise, yet he thought
"no man of a cultivated understanding,
"should dedicate his *whole* time to the sports
"of the field." I remember, this remark at
the time, gave me great offence, because it

was

was manifeſtly directed at me, but I have ſince conſidered, it might imply a compliment to my underſtanding, and rejoice in the opportunity I have had of being convinced he meant it as ſuch. He calls on me every day ſince my illneſs, and when I reflect on the contraſt betwixt his converſation, and that of my former companions, I am confounded at my inſenſibility and blindneſs to my own intereſt. On Thurſday evening laſt, my neighbour, JACK TOPALL, ſat half an hour with me, when he related all the events of the preceding day, " where they had thrown off— " where the fox broke cover—where the " hounds were at fault—how old Ringwood " clapt on him—the burſt of fifteen miles " right out—who were in at the death, and " at laſt, that the whole concluded with two " bottles a man, beſides ſpirits and white " wine." I went to bed heated with the deſcription, dreamed of leaping five barred gates, broke my leg again and again, and woke with all the ſymptoms of having taken my ſhare of the wine after the chace; nor could I ſhake off the effects of my friend JACK's converſation, till the good Vicar called on me, and gave a new turn to my thoughts. From horſes and dogs he led them

to men and things; for without the least appearance of pedantry, he insensibly conducts
me to subjects of Literature, and flatters
my understanding, by appealing to its decisi-
on; we yesterday read your last paper together, and he pointed out the happy metaphor at the conclusion, where you allude
to the *Mountain of Calamity*; he observed that
the SPECTATOR had said something of the
same kind, where he compares " the evils of
" this life to rocks and precipices, which ap-
" pear rugged and barren at a distance, but at
" our nearer approach, we find little fruitful
" spots and refreshing springs, mixed with
" the harshness and deformities of nature."

WITH my mind engaged in this contemplation, I went to rest, when the following
dream produced such vivid imagery to my
fancy, that I almost doubt whether I was
asleep, or only musing and commenting on
your metaphor; I conceived myself tran-
sported to a delightful country, beautifully
variegated with gentle hills and vales, with
woods and plains and cultivated fields, which
were for ever changing as I passed on;
for TIME, who was my Conductor, never
would give me leave to stop a minute in
a place, except when sleep made me insensi-
ble,

ble of his progreſſive motion: for then he
would gently carry me in his arms to ſome
ſpot which commanded nearly the ſame proſpect with that, where wearineſs had over-
taken me; but I would not have you fancy
my conductor was an old man with a ſcythe
and an hour glaſs, as he is generally repre-
ſented, no; he was continually changing
ſhapes; when I firſt met him he was a healthy
playful boy, he taught me many a puerile
game, and cheered my firſt ſteps with paſtimes
and delights, we danced rather than walked
the beginning of our journey, for all was
ſport and feſtive innocence; at length he led
me by the hand through Academic Groves,
where every ſtep we took, enlarged my
proſpects and increaſed my ſatisfaction in his
company. I had only one cauſe of diſcontent,
and that was, as I before hinted, that he never
would permit me to ſtop a minute in a place,
or go back to view the ſcenes which had given
me the greateſt pleaſure; indeed he would
ſometimes give a reaſon for his non-compli-
ance, by telling me, " that the delight
" of every ſcene conſiſted chiefly in its no-
" velty," and he would ſometimes ſhew me
the picture of the places I had viſited, reflected in the *Mirror of Experience*, which
confirmed-

confirmed the truth of what he faid. On my
departure from the Academic Grove, I was
ftruck with the appearance of a vaft extenfive
plain, a fort of heath or common, interfected
by many roads, but which all feemed to tend
towards an object I had never before beheld ;
it was a diftant mountain, whofe bleak and
barren afpect, at once convinced me that
it was the *Mountain of Calamity*; I fhrunk
from the fight, and would have gladly turned
back into the Grove, or at leaft wifhed to
ftop and refolve which of the roads it were
moft advifeable to take, but my conductor
hurried me on, bidding me not direct my eyes
to painful objects at a diftance, but look
about me; I did fo, and was again delighted
with the profpect near at hand, the ground
was enamelled with a thoufand flowers, that
fhed their fweets as we paffed by; I faw
before me at a little diftance the moft delightful objects, through which the feveral roads
feemed to take their refpective courfes; one
led through a *City*, whofe Palaces glittered
with riches, the effect of *Trade*; another led
to a fplendid Fane, dedicated to *Naval* and
Military Honours; another to a Sacred Grove,
where *Holy* Contemplation feemed to enfure
Peace and Happinefs; and others ftill thro'

various

various interesting scenes; each was surrounded with enchanting prospects, but each
was more or less exposed to a view of the diftant *Mountain*; and I observed, that in proportion as the inhabitants of these several
places, struggled to ascend to the highest
spots of their situation, they had a more diftinct view of the Mountain which all wished
to shun : struck with this reflection, I chose
a road different from any I have mentioned,
and passed through villages and pleasant
farms, where unexpected scenery on every
side delighted me; I could often view detached
parts of all the other roads, and sometimes
travelled a few miles in each; but though my
prospects on each side were ever varying, and
always pleasant, yet I could not avoid a sight
of the fearful Mountain, and this as I approached it nearer, seemed to rob the sur-
rounding landscapes of their charms, and by
degrees, I found my spirits sinking, and
became disgusted with my journey. Sometimes my conductor would bid me take courage, and enjoy with him the nearer prospects, or look back on the country we
had passed; there I saw some hills which
I had climbed with ease, and some which
I had avoided without knowing how : I was

often

often pleafed to fee torrents which I had
paffed without danger, and fometimes vexed
to perceive objects that I had miffed, and
to which now there was no going back ; by
thus looking round occafionally, I infenfibly
preffed forward till I was fo near the Mountain, that it feemed impoffible to remove it
from my eyes ; but how was I overwhelmed
with defpair at the horrors of my way, when
on a fudden, a few fteps farther prefented the
full profpect of the *River of Death*, which
fwept away thoufands in their paffage to
the Mountain; nay, I faw fome volunta-
rily plunge into the waves, rather than look
forward ; but my conductor recommended
me to *Fortitude*, who leading me through
the bye-path of *Difficulty*, I began to afcend
the Mountain ; and now I perceived it lefs
barren than I dreaded, the roads were rugged
indeed, but the view from thence of the
country I had paffed, was often not unpleaf-
ing; the river at the foot of the hill had loft
its terrors, though from the plains of Happinefs it was a dreadful object ; I could trace its
courfe and faw with aftonifhment, that it
wandered through the whole extent of the
journey I had taken, and that many who purfued the feveral tracks, were often deftroyed.

by

by the rapid torrent, in the moſt unexpected
part of their progreſs to that Mountain which
they ſaw but never reached.   As I was
earneſtly ſurveying the many places where I
had myſelf eſcaped, I ſtruck my bruiſed knee
againſt a projecting rock, and woke with the
pain, and while the viſion is ſtill freſh, I have
ſent it you, and ſhall be happy if it furniſhes
your readers with *Variety*.

I am, &c.

VENATOR QUONDAM.

NUM-

N U M B E R   XV.

HAVING been reproached by a young female correspondent, for my silence on the subject of LOVE, I have for some time past been employed in collecting materials to oblige her, from observations in the circle of my acquaintance; but at length a friend assured me, that I might as well attempt to describe a *Griffin*, or a *Unicorn*; "for LOVE," says he, "like these monsters, is a thing which "may possibly have existed in former times, "but *now* mankind are wiser than to believe "any thing of the matter." I shall consider this as the opinion only of an old man who has forgot what he felt himself when he was young; and proceed to give a very singular instance of affection betwixt two Lovers *who never saw each other.*

THIS

THIS curious fact I have extracted from a manuscript in a dialect of the Persian language, and shall give it to my readers, partly as a translation, and partly as an abstract from a more extended narrative.

THE HISTORY OF

TAREMPOU AND SERINDA.

" IT was on the banks of the sonorous
" river *Tsampu*, whose thundering cataracts
" refresh the burning foil, and sometimes
" shake the mighty mountains which divide
" Thibet from the empire of Mogul ; there
" lived a wealthy and revered LAMA, whose
" lands were tributary to the SUPREME
" LAMA, or SACERDOTAL EMPEROR, who
" governs all the land from China to the
" pathless desert of Cobi : but although his
" flocks and herds were scattered over an
" hundred hills, and the number of his slaves
" exceeded the breathings of man's life, yet
" was he chiefly known throughout all the
" East, as *the father of Serinda*.   It was the
" beauty, the virtue, the accomplishments of
" Serinda, which gave him all his fame,
" and all his happiness; for LAMA *Zarin*
" considered the advantages which birth and
weal-

" wealth and power conferred, as trifling
" when compared to that of being *father to*
" *Serinda.* All the anxiety he ever felt, pro-
" ceeded from the thoughts relating to
" her welfare, when he could no longer
" guard the innocence of *her*, whom he ex-
" pected foon to quit for ever." A dreadful
malady, which had long feized him at a ftated
hour each day, he found was gaining on him,
and threatened, in fpite of all the arts of medicine, to put a fpeedy period to his exiftence.

One day after a fit, which attacked him with
more violence than ufual, he fent for the fair
Serinda, and gently beckoning her to approach
his couch, he addreffed her in thefe words:
" Daughter of my hopes and fears! Heaven
" grant that thou mayeft fmile for ever! Yet
" while my foul confeffes its delight in gaz-
" ing on thee, attend to the foreboding me-
" lancholy dictates of a dying father's
" fpirit: my *Serinda*, whofe breath refreshes
" like the rofe, and whofe purity fhould like
" the jeffamine, diffufe voluptuous fatisfacti-
" on all around her, difturbs the peace of he
" dejected father, embittering all the com
" forts of his life, and making his approach
" to death more terrible." At thefe words
Serinda, unconfcious of offence, and doubting
wha

what she heard, fell on her knees, and urged
her father to explain his meaning ; while he,
gently raising her, proceeded thus, " the
" Angel of Death, who admonishes and
" warns the faithful in the hour of sickness,
" 'ere he strikes the fatal blow, has summon-
" ed me to join thy holy mother, who died
" when she gave birth to my *Serinda*; yet let
" me not depart to the unknown and fearful
" Land of Death, and leave my daughter un-
" protected ; Oh ! my *Serinda*, speak ! Hast
" thou ever seriously reflected on the danger,
" to which thy orphan state must soon be sub-
" ject ; surrounded as thou then wilt be with
" suitor LAMAS, of various dispositions and
" pretensions; some with mercenary cunning,
" wooeing thy possessions through thy person;
" others haughtily demanding both, and
" threatening a helpless heiress with their pow-
" erful love ;" he then reminded her that he
had from time to time presented her with por-
raits of the several Princes or LAMAS, who
had solicited an union with his house, and
which they had sent according to the custom
of *Thibet*, where the sexes can never see each
ther till they are married ; he also repeated
what he had already himself given her in
writing, an epitome of their characters, their

G

good

good and evil qualities, their ages, their po
feffions, and their rank in the Priefthood
the LAMA, and concluded by faying, " te
" me then, my *Serinda*, which of all the
" mighty Princes can claim a preference
" the foul of my beloved daughter?" *Serin*
blufhed and fighed, but anfwered not—LAM
Zarin defired that fhe would withdraw
confult the paper he had given her, to con
pare it with the feveral portraits, and dete
mine before his next day's fit returned, whi
might be moft deferving of her love.   At
word LOVE, *Serinda* blufhed again, but kne
not why,—her father faw the crimfon on h
cheek, but faid it was the timid flufhing of
virgin's modefty, and urged her to withdra
and to be quick in her decifion; *Serin*
with innocence replied, " my father kno
" that he is himfelf the only man I ever fa
" and I think the only being I can ev
" *love*, at leaft my *love* will ever be confin
" to thofe objects which delight or benefit
" father, whether they be man or beaft;
" I *love* this favourite dog, which my fath
" fo frequently careffes; I *loved* the favour
" horfe on which my father rode, till
" a fall he put his mafter's life in dang,
" then I hated him; but when the tyger
                                           " feiz

" feized my father on the ground, and he was
" delivered by his trufty flave, I *loved Tarem-*
" *pou*; and fince my father daily acknow-
" ledges that he faved his life, I *love Tarem-*
" *pou* ftill." The father heard her artlefs
confeffion, and told her that *Tarempou* was no
LAMA; " but," faid fhe, " which of all
" thofe LAMAS who now demand my love,
" has made an intereft in my heart by fervices
" to my father, like the flave *Tarempou?*
" And yet I have not feen his perfon or his
" picture, nor know I whether he be old
" or young; but he has faved my father's
" life, and is a favourite of my father, there-
" fore it is my duty fure to *love*, and I will
" *love Tarempou*." The old LAMA fmiling,
gently rebuked his daughter for the freedom
of her expreffion, and defired her to withdraw,
after he had explained to her that *love* was *im-*
pious according to the laws of *Thibet*, betwixt
any of the race of LAMAS and their flaves;
Scrinda left her father, and as fhe ftroked his
favourite dog which lay at the door of his
apartment, a tear trembled in her eye, left fhe
might be guilty of *impiety*.

AND now the flave *Tarempou*, who for his
fervices had been advanced from Chief of the
Shepherds, to be Chief of the Houfhold,

G 2

had

had an audience of his master; and observing him unusually dejected, declared that he had himself acquired some knowledge in medicine, and humbly begged permission to try his skill where every other attempt had proved unsuccessful. The LAMA heard his proposal with a mixture of pleasure and contempt; or, as 'tis expressed in the original, "his eyes flashed joy, "his brow looked forgiveness, but contempt "and incredulity smiled upon his lips, while "his tongue answered the faithful *Tarempou* "in gratitude and doubt." The slave replied, "may LAMA *Zarin* live for ever "I boast no secret antidote, no mystic "charm to work a sudden miracle; be "I have been taught in Europe the gradua "effects of alterative medicines; 'tis from "these alone that I expect to gain in time b "perseverance, a compleat victory over th "disease; and if in seven days time th "smallest change encourage me to persevere "I will then boldly look forward, and eithe "die or conquer." The Prince assented; an from that day became the patient of *Tarem pou*, whose situation both as Chief in th house, and as Physician, gave him a right t be at all times in the LAMA's presence, fav

whe

when *Serinda* paid her daily vifit to her father, and then he had notice to withdraw.

THE firſt week had not elapſed before the LAMA was convinced that his diſeaſe gave way to the medicines of his favourite: the fits returned indeed, but every day they attacked him with leſs violence, and were of ſhorter duration. In proportion as *Tarempou* became leſs neceſſary as a phyſician, his company became more deſirable as a friend; he poſſeſſed a lively imagination, and had improved his natural good underſtanding by travel in diſtant countries: thus his converſation often turned on ſubjeẟs which were quite new to the delighted LAMA; they talked of laws, religion, and cuſtoms of foreign kingdoms, comparing them with thoſe of *Thibet*; and by degrees the ſlave became the friend, and almoſt equal of his maſter: amongſt other topics of diſcourſe, the LAMA would often tell of the virtues and endowments of his beloved daughter, while *Tarempou* liſtened with delight, and felt an intereſt in the ſubjeẟ which he was at a loſs himſelf to comprehend. On the other hand, in the converſations of the LAMA with *Serinda*, he could talk of nothing but the ſkill and wiſdom of *Tarempou*, wondering at ſuch various knowledge in ſo young a man.

G 3

IT

IT happened one day when he had been repeating to his daughter, the account *Ta-rempou* gave of European manners, that *Serinda* blushed and sighed; her father asked the cause, when she ingenuously confessed, that he had so often mentioned this young slave, that she could think of nothing else by day or night; and that in her dreams she saw him, and thought he was a LAMA worthy of her *love*; then turning to her father with artless innocence, she said, " Oh LAMA, tell me! can my *sleep* be *impious?* Her father saw her with emotion, and told her she must think of him no more. " I will endeavour to obey," she said, "but I shall dream, and sleep will " *impiously* restore my banished waking " thoughts." The LAMA dreading the flame he had himself kindled in his daughter's bosom, endeavoured to check her rising passion, and resolved, thenceforth, never again to tell her of the slave *Tarempou*; but now it was too late, *love* of the purest kind had taken full possession of the virgin's heart, and while she struggled to obey her father, the fierce contention betwixt this unknown guest, and the dread of being *impious*, prey'd upon her health, till feverish days and sleep-

lefs

lefs nights at length expofed, her life to danger.

IT was impoffible for LAMA *Zarin* to conceal from *Tarempou* (whom we will now no longer call his flave, but his faithful *friend*) the ficknefs of *Serinda*; and while he confeffed his alarm for his fair daughter's fafety, he plainly faw that he had too often defcribed that daughter to his favourite : he faw what it was impoffible for *Tarempou* to conceal, that he had been the fatal caufe of mutual paffion to two lovers who had never feen, and but for him could never have heard of each others amiable qualities Thus fituated, (even if the laws of *Thibet* had permitted the vifit of a male phyfician) prudence would have forbid his employing the only fkill in which he now had confidence ; but *Serinda*, whofe difeafe was occafionally attended with delirium, would only call upon the name of *Tarempou*, often repeating, " he faved my " father, and it is he alone can fave the lin- " gering *Serinda*."

OVERCOME by the intreaties of his love-fick daughter, the afflicted father, in an agony of grief, curfed the cruel laws of *Thibet*, and told her, " fhe fhould fee *Tarem-* " *pou*." *Serinda* heard with extacy, and

knowing

knowing that what a LAMA promises, must
ever be performed, the words became a bal-
sam to the wounds of *love*: but the LAMA
had not fixed the time when his sacred pro-
mise should be fulfilled ; nor would he, till
he had withdrawn and weighed the consequence of what had fallen from his lips.
The oftener he revolved the subject in his
thoughts, the less appeared the difficulties ;
and having by his conversations with *Tarempou*, raised his mind above the slavish preju-
dices and customs of his country ; he at
length resolved to overcome all scruples, and
to give his beloved daughter to the only man
whom he thought worthy of her.

FULL of the idea of their future happiness,
he determined to obtain all that remained necessary for its completion, which was, the
sanction of that higher power to which all
the LAMAS of *Thibet* are subject : he instantly dispatched messengers to the GREAT LA-
MA, who resides at *Tonker*, with whom his
influence was so great, that he had no doubt
he should obtain whatever he might ask, although unprecedented in the laws of *Thibet* ;
laws which forbid the *holy race* of LAMAS to
intermarry with any but of their own Sacred
Order. And now unable to suppress the joy

he

he felt in communicating to the lovers, that plan of future blifs which he had formed, he raifed *Tarempou* to a pitch of hope which neither his love nor his ambition had ever dared to cherifh ; and to *Serinda* he promifed that the fight of her phyfician and her lover, fhould only be deferred one week, or till the meffenger returned from the GREAT LAMA at *Tonker*.

FROM this day the phyfician was no longer neceffary : but the week appeared a tedious age to the expecting love of young *Tarempou*, and his promifed bride *Serinda*.

NUMBER XVI.

I AM willing to fuppofe that fome of my tender hearted Readers may have fympathized with the Lovers, who have been left to endure a week's expectation and fufpence, and fhall now procced with the Narrative.

THE HISTORY OF

TAREMPOU AND SERINDA,

CONTINUED.

THE feven days at length elapfed, when the meffenger returned from *Tonker*, with the following anfwer: " *The* " *moft facred Sultan, the mighty* SOVEREIGN " LAMA, *who enjoyeth life for ever, and at* " *whofe nod a thoufand Princes perifh or revive,* "- *fendeth to* LAMA *Zarin, greeting.   Report* " *has long made known at Tonker, the beauty of* " *Serinda,*

" *Serinda, and by thy meſſenger we learn, the*
" *matchleſs excellence of thy ſlave Tarempou. In*
" *anſwer, therefore, to thy requeſt, that theſe may*
" *be united, mark the purpoſe of our Sovereign*
" *Will, which, not to obey is death, throughout*
" *the realms of Thibet. The lovers ſhall not ſee*
" *each other, till they both ſtand before the ſacred*
" *footſteps of our Throne at Tonker, that we our-*
" *ſelves in perſons, may witneſs the emotion*
" *of their amorous ſouls."*

THIS anſwer, far from removing the ſuſ-
pence, created one a thouſand times more terrible. The LAMA-*Zarin*, thought it portended ruin to himſelf and family ; he now reflected on the raſh ſteps he had taken, and
feared his ſanguine hopes had been deceived
by frequent converſations with a ſtranger,
who had taught him to think lightly of
the laws and cuſtoms of *Thibet*, for which he
now recollected with horror, the GREAT
LAMA's bigotry and zeal ; he knew he muſt
obey the ſummons, and trembled at his ſituation. *Tarempou* was too much enamoured to
think of any danger which promiſed him
a ſight of his beloved miſtreſs ; and all the fear
he felt, was, leſt the beauty of *Serinda* ſhould
tempt the SUPREME LAMA, to ſeize her for
himſelf. " But *ſhe*, in whoſe love-ſick heart,

G 6

" dwelt

" dwelt pureſt Innocence, a fountain from
" whence ſprang Hope, which branching in
" a thouſand channels, diffuſed itſelf over all
" her ſoul, and gleamed in her countenance,
" half ſeen and half concealed, like the mean-
" dering veins that ſweetly overſpread her
" ſwelling boſom ;" revered the LAMA for his
decree, and thought it proceeded from his deſire of being witneſs to the mutual happineſs
of virtuous love: with theſe ſentiments ſhe
felt only joy at their departure, which took
place that very day with all the pomp and retinue of Eaſtern ſplendour.

HERE in the original follows a very long
detail of their journey, deſcribing the number
of their attendants, with the camels and ele-
phants employed on the occaſion ; it relates
that the LAMA would ſometimes travel in the
ſumptuous palanquin of his daughter, and
ſometimes rode on the ſame elephant with
Tarempou, dividing his time betwixt the converſation of each, but unable to ſuppreſs his
apprehenſions or diſſipate the fears of his foreboding mind. To compreſs the ſtory within
the limits of this paper, I ſhall immediately
proceed to the Tribunal which was held
in the great HALL OF SILENCE, and
leave the reader to imagine the magnificence,
which

which there is not now room to defcribe
at large. At the upper end of the fuperb
apartment, fat on a throne of maffy gold, the
SUPREME LAMA; before him at fome diftance were two altars fmoaking with fragrant
incenfe, and around him knelt an hundred
LAMAS, in filent adoration (for in *Thibet*
all men pay divine honours to the SUPREME
LAMA, who is fuppofed to live for ever,
the fame fpirit paffing from father to fon) to
this folemn Tribunal, LAMA *Zarin* was introduced by Mufes, from an apartment
directly oppofite to the Throne, and knelt in
awful filence betwixt the fmoaking altars—
at the fame time from two doors facing each
other, were ufhered in *Tarempou* and *Serinda*,
each covered by a thick veil, which was faftened to the fummit of their turbans, and
touched the ground, and each accompanied by
a Mute fell proftrate before the Throne—
a dreadful ftillnefs now prevailed—all was
mute as death—while doubt, fufpence, and
horror, chilled the bofoms of the expecting
Lovers—in this fearful interval of filence, the
throbbing of *Serinda*'s heart, became diftinctly
audible, and pierced the foul of her *Tarempou*—the father heard it too; and a half-
fmothered figh involuntarily ftole from his

bofom

bofom, and refounded through the echo-
ing dome—at length, the folemn deep toned
voice of the GREAT LAMA, uttered thefe
words: " Attend! and mark the will of HIM
" who fpeaks with the *mouth of Heaven*;
" arife! and hear! Know, that the promife
" of a LAMA is facred as the words of
" ALLA; therefore are ye brought hither to
" behold each other, and in this auguft pre-
" fence, by a folemn union, to receive the
" reward of love, which a fond father's praife
" has kindled in your fouls, and which
" he having promifed, muft be fulfilled:
" Prepare to remove the veils. Let LAMA
" *Zarin* join your hands, and then embrace
" each other; but on your lives, utter not a
" word; for know, that in the *Hall of*
" *Silence*, 'tis death for any tongue to found,
" but that which fpeaks the *Voice of*
" *Heaven*."

HE ceafed,—and his words refounding from
the lofty roof, gradually died upon the ear till
the fame dreadful ftillnefs again prevailed
through all the building;—and now, at a
fignal given,—the Mutes removed the veils
at the fame moment, and difcovered the
beauteous perfons of *Tarempou* and *Serinda*.
What language can defcribe the matchlefs

grace

grace of each, far less convey an adequate idea of that expreffion, with which each beheld the other in agonies of joy, fufpence and rapture; but they gazed in filence, till by another fignal from the throne, the father joined their hands, and then *Tarempou*, as commanded, embraced his lovely bride; while fhe, unable to fupport this trying moment, fainted in his arms;—and now, *Tarempou*, regardlefs of the prohibition, exclaimed, "help! my *Serinda dies*." Inftantly the voice from the throne returned this melancholy found: "*Tarempou dies*;" immediately two mutes approached with the fatal bow-ftring, and feizing *Tarempou*, fixed an inftrument of filence on his lips;—while other Mutes hurried away *Serinda*, infenfible to the danger of her lover; but the father, unable to reftrain the anguifh of his foul, cried out with bitternefs. " If to fpeak, be death, " let me die alfo; but firft, I will execrate " the favage cuftoms, and curfe the laws " that doom the innocent." He would have proceeded, but other Mutes furrounded him, and ftopped his fpeech, as they had done *Tarempou*'s. Then the SUPREME LAMA again addreffed them in thefe words: " Know, " prefumptuous and devoted wretches, that

" before

" before ye brake that folemn law which en-
" joins filence in this facred prefence, ye
" were already doomed to death. Thou,
" LAMA *Zarin*, for daring to degrade the
" Holy Priefthood of LAMAS by marrying
" thy daughter to a flave ; and thou, *Tarem-*
" *pou*, for prefuming to ally thyfelf with one
" of that Sacred Race ; the promife which
" this foolifh LAMA made, was literally
" fulfilled, thefe daring rebels againft the
" laws of *Thibet*, have feen, and been united
" to each other ; and the embrace which
" was permitted, was doomed to be the laft ;
" Now, therefore, Mutes perform your of-
" fice on *Tarempou* firft." They according-
ly bound the victim, who was already
gagged, to one of the altars, and were fixing
the cord about his neck, when they defifted
on a fudden, and proftrating themfelves before *Tarempou*, they performed the fame obei-
fance, which is paid only to the heir of the
facred throne of *Tonker*. A general confternation feized all prefent ; and the SUPREME
LAMA defcending from his throne, approached *Tarempou* ; on whofe left fhoulder,
which had been uncovered by the execu-
tioners, he now perceived the myftic characters, with which the facred family of *Thibet*

are

are always diſtinguiſhed at their birth.   He ſaw the well known mark, the voice of nature confirmed this teſtimony of his ſight, and falling on the neck of *Tarempou*, he exclaimed, " It is my ſon ! my long loſt ſon ! " quickly reſtore his voice, henceforth this " place ſhall be no longer called the *Hall of* " *Silence*, but of *Joy* ; for in this place, we " will to-morrow celebrate the nuptials of. " *Tarempou* and *Serinda*."

THE Hiſtory then explains this ſudden event, by relating that ſome Jeſuit Miſſionaries, who had gained acceſs to the capital of *Thibet*, in their zeal for religion, had ſtolen the heir of the throne, then an infant, hoping to make uſe of him in the converſion of theſe people ; but in their retreat through the great deſart of Cobi, they had been attacked by a banditti, who killed the Jeſuits, and ſold the young Lama for a ſlave ; he had ſerved in the Ottoman army; he had been taken by the Knights of Malta ; afterwards became ſervant to a French officer with whom he travelled through all Europe, and at length accompanied him to India ; here in an engagement with the Mahrattas, he had been again taken priſoner, and ſold as a ſlave to ſome merchants of *Thibet* ; by this

means

means he came into the service of LAMA
Zarin, without knowing any thing of his
origin, or the meaning of those characters
which he bore on his left shoulder, and
which had effected this wonderful difcovery.

THE Hiftory concludes with faying, that
Tarempou was wedded to the fair *Serinda* ; and
that their happinefs was unexampled : that
the leffons he had been taught in the fchool of
adverfity, and the obfervations he had made
in the various countries he had feen, prepared
him to abolifh the many foolifh and impious
cuftoms of *Thibet* ; and he caufed to be
written over the *Throne* of the GREAT HALL,
this Infcription.

   " MARK the Cries of Diftrefs, and
" give Relief.—Receive the Bleffings
" of the grateful, and rejoice in them.
" —Hearken to the Words of Age,
" Experience and Goodnefs, and obey
" them.—Stifle not the feelings of
" Humanity, but encourage virtuous
" Love ; for the ftill fmall Voice of
" Innocence and Nature, is in every
" Country the true *Voice of Heaven*."

NUM-

N U M B E R   XVII.

THE fubject I have chofen for this day's
effay, is of fo facred a nature, that I
feel an awful tremor at my own prefumption
while I write, and am at a lofs to defcribe
the reverence with which I think upon it.
I have the authority of my great predeceffor
the SPECTATOR, for occafionally blending
with trivial topics, Effays on the moft exalted fubjects ; and am led to the choice I
have now made, by a perufal of No. 531, in
that matchlefs Collection: it is there obferved and confirmed by the opinion of Mr.
LOCKE, that we form our ideas of the Su-
PREME BEING, by taking whatever we deem
excellent in our own nature, and adding to
it the idea of *Infinity.* Thus we know that
" *we* exift in place and time. The *Divine*
" *Being*

" *Being* fills all space, and inhabits eternity.
" *We* are possessed of a little power and a
" little knowledge. The *Divine Being* is *Al-*
" *mighty* and *Omniscient* ; in short, by adding
" infinity to any kind of perfection we en-
" joy, and by joining all these different
" kinds of perfections in ONE BEING, we
" form our idea of the *Great Sovereign of*
" *Nature.*"   But he does not reflect, that of
infinity we have no idea. We often use words
without meaning, and this is the case with
almost every attribute we have annexed to the
Deity : for example, *Eternal* and *Omnipotent*
can only mean of *long duration* and *very*
powerful ; no man thinks of Eternity but by
the help of adding certain periods of *Time* together, without considering that *Time* can never
be the measure of *Eternity* : for if we multiply
a million of years, by a million of years, ten
thousand times together, we shall be as wide
of any comparative knowledge of *Eternity*, as
if we had rested at the first unit. Since
millions of years deducted from *Eternity*,
cannot make it shorter by a single second ;
indeed, to talk of such a deduction, is an
absurdity and contradiction in language, like
that we use in saying, for ever and ever, as
if *Eternity* could be doubled.   Therefore, of
the

the divine attribute *Eternal*, we have really
no other idea, but that of a long duration of
exiftence; the period of which, is to us un-
intelligible and incomprehenfible.

IN like manner, *Omnipotence* cannot be
conceived by man, but under certain limit-
ations and reftrictions; we know that two
and two make four, and cannot allow
that any degree of power, with which we
are at prefent acquainted, could make it
otherwife: yet a man would be deemed impious, who fhould deny this power in *Omnipotence*, although the acknowledgement of it,
is contradictory to common fenfe.

IN the fame imperfect manner do we fpeak
of all the other attributes. We talk of *perfect Juftice* and *perfect Mercy*, without confidering that they cannot exift together; for
Mercy can never be exercifed, but at the expence of rigid *Juftice*. How oppofite to the
true meaning of words are *indignation*, *anger*,
and *difpleafure*, when applied to a Being un-
changeably, and fupremely perfect in *love*,
in goodnefs, and in *happinefs*; it appears to me
therefore, that we are guilty of folly, if not of
impiety, in affixing attributes to that BEING,
whofe nature and properties are not to be
comprehended by human reafon; and indeed,

the

the consequence of forming a judgment, on
so mysterious a subject, has been, that men
have not only attributed to GOD, their own
excellencies and virtues, but even their
passions, vices, and irregularities.   The
Savage sees in the Being which he worships,
vengeance and *terror*, with all the fiery passions that agitate his own ungovernable soul.
The *Turk*, whose greatest mental enjoyment
consists in rest, from thoughts and cares,
conceives that the GREAT ALLA, is su-
premely happy in everlasting quiet.   The
Brachman, whose steady contemplation is
sometimes fixed for years on the same object,
and who subdues and stifles all the finer feelings of humanity, by habits of abstrusest
thought; supposes that the Deity is absorbed
in contemplation of those attributes, which
are so far beyond the comprehension of the
most enlightened human intelligence.

THE wisest of the ancients have not hesitated to worship as Gods, every human passion,
whether good or evil; and paid their adoration to a God of Wine, a God of Love, a
God of War; and fifty others of the like
kind: nor did they stop here; for having
endued their Gods with passions like themselves, they gave them wives, and sons, and
daughters,

daughters, with all the relations which most intimately connect mortals to each other; deducing genealogies from antient records, in which they mistook figurative expressions, and allegorical allusions, for literal descriptions and matter of fact. Such has been the absurdity of all ages, when speaking of what is so infinitely beyond all human scrutiny. The more a wise man contemplates the GREAT CREATOR of all things, the more is he conscious of his own insignificance and inability, to think rationally on so incomprehensible a subject. And here my readers will thank me, for transcribing a beautiful passage from a living author, who speaks thus reverently of the all-wife, and all-powerful Divinity: " But of HIM, the great *first* " *Cause!* The Principle of all Principles ! " Of HIM, from whom the whole Universe, " and all that it contains, derive their prin- " ciples ; what shall we say, or how, speak " with propriety ? So weak, so incompetent, " are we, that we are lost in the contem- " plation of his nature, and hardly know " how to discourse of him with tolerable " sense, or without absurdity, and danger " of impiety and profanation."

THE

THE *Omnipresence*, or ubiquity of the *Deity*, though involved in much difficulty has been more happily illustrated, and i better understood, than any other attribute We see in all the works of nature, something that brings conviction of the influence which produces and sustains. We see in plants, a power of vegetation which acts with uniformity, although we know not how. In the animal world, whether we survey the production, the growth, the motions, or that instinctive love of happiness, by which every individual seems actuated; we are at a glance convinced, that there is something more than *matter* operating in them. But when we reflect on man; when we feel that internal satisfaction or disgust at what appears good or evil in our natures; we cannot deny, that there is something besides ourselves, condemning or applauding all our thoughts and actions. In short, which ever way we turn our eyes, we see an influence beyond our comprehension, and perceive effects, altho the cause remains invisible; yet knowing that there can be no effect without a cause, it must be GOD; who

" ——Chang'

" — Chang'd thro' all, and yet in all the fame,
" Great in the earth, as in the ætherial frame;
" Warm in the fun, refrefhes in the breeze,
" Glows in the ftars, and bloffoms in the trees;
" Lives thro' all life, extends thro' all extent,
" Spreads undivided, operates unfpent;
" Breathes in our foul, informs our mortal part,
" As full, as perfect, in a *hair*, *as heart*."

Let us not then attempt to defcribe what we cannot comprehend, or give names, and attributes, and qualities of our own, which degrade the Great Creator; let us always fpeak and even think with the utmoft reverence, of a *Name*, which among the Gentoo Indians, is never mentioned but in a whifper; for none of the moft holy amongft he priefts, would prefume to pronounce iloud, the myftic name of the Most High- ist; while we who boaft a more genuine eligion, profane it in the ftreets on the moft rivial occafions; rather let us with gratitude cknowledge all his benefits, without pre- iming to limit his influence or favour to any articular fect, or opinion   We are told

H   in

in a book of the higheſt antiquity, tha
" to do juſtice, to love mercy, and to wall
" humbly before GOD, are the things moſ
" acceptable in his ſight."

NUM

N U M B E R   XVIII.

SIR,

IT has been the cant of all writers, and particularly of your predeceffors, to de-claim againft *Diffipation*, but few have de-fined in what it confifts; indeed the defini-tion might prove dangerous to themfelves; for I have fometimes confidered even *writing itfelf* to be one fpecies of it; at leaft, I have often fat me down to write letters, becaufe a rainy day has confined me to the houfe, when I have neither had a new book to read, nor a new acquaintance to talk with; that, Sir, is the cafe at this prefent moment, I have literally " nothing to do, and can't fleep." Therefore, having been revolving the fubject of Diffipation in my mind, I will unburthen my thoughts to you, and you may empty hem out into the world, either muddy as I

H 2

fend

send them, or strain them through your sieve as if they had passed the Academy *de la Crusca*.

WHAT a jumble of contradictions is man, this mighty lord of the creation! the more I consider his nature, the more I am inclined to believe you to be right, in saying that his love of Variety distinguishes him more than any other quality from his brutal fellow animals; for no man living can exist with perfect sameness of objects, or pursuits. The Horse enjoys life seemingly without discontent, if he be regularly fed, and cleaned, and watered; and will remain whole days and weeks in the same stall, without a struggle to get loose, if you supply him with his necessary food; for though he may display his courage in the battle, his ardour in the chase, and even emulation in the course, and seems to share his rider's energy in all his danger, or his sports; yet he would never unsolicited, neglect the crib and stable to join the scene of action. The same may be observed of all the animals whose services belong to man; nor do the more savage beasts of prey appear inclined to leave their dreary homes, but when impelled by nature to satisfy

tisfy the calls of hunger, or more powerful stimulants to action. But Man, whose boasted Reason seems to fit him for a state of rest and quiet contemplation, is for ever anxious to dispel that faculty by which he claims superior rank in the creation.

The slightest consideration of our acquaintance, and view of their pursuits, will amply elucidate my observation; but this remark does not extend to those who have *no thought to dissipate:* thus, although Aristotle has defined man to be an "animal which walks "erect upon two legs, and has no feathers;" yet that is not the definition of a Rational Being: there are thousands of human beings in the world which are but one degree above mere brutes; and some which ought not to be compared with the Horse in point of understanding. Men who rise at a certain hour each day, are worked a certain time like cattle, or work themselves, ('tis the same thing) and having been fed, and rested, at certain intervals, are summoned to a fresh day's labour without Variety of thought, or occupation: nor do I mean to condemn them as less useful beings, but they should not be confounded with the more enlightened of their fellow creatures; with those, whose

H 3 minds

minds have been enlarged by education, and improved by travel and ſtudy ; who are not compelled to earn their daily bread with toil and ſorrow, but who employ their reaſoning powers, ſometimes in collecting thought, but oftener in its Diſſipation, while they condemn in others, habits which they diſlike themſelves.

Sir Robert Rackett, who began his education at Eaton, and finiſhed it at Oxford, condemns his lady's *diſſipation*. Her ladyſhip, whoſe manners were poliſhed at the moſt expenſive boarding-ſchool near town, divides her winter amidſt the ſweet Variety of operas, maſquerades, routs, drums, and faſhionable parties ; ſhe is a woman of too much good ſenſe to enjoy this conſtant ſucceſſion of what others call amuſement, for any real pleaſures they afford ; for without novelty, they looſe their charms to pleaſe ; but what can ſhe do elſe ? ſhe hates reflection, though it is free from guilt. Sir Robert, on the other hand, drags on his time betwixt a ſaunter in Hyde-Park, a game at tennis, or the converſation of the grooms at Tatterſall's ; dines at a tavern, and hating cards, returns to his own houſe half drunk about the time her ladyſhip prepares to ſally

forth ;

forth ; while she slips out another way, to a-
void the ill-timed meeting. When soberly,
he asks himself the cause of this strange
waste of life, he confesses he has no enjoyment in it ; but that like Lady Rackett, he
must do something to fill up his time. In the
country, her ladyship breeds poultry, and
saunters in the grounds without delight, or
thrums her harpsichord without an ear, because
she must do something till the time comes
for her return to London. While the Baronet is planting without improvement, or
hunting without glee ; not because he is a
man of taste, or a keen sportsman, but because any thing is better than staying in the
house and *muzzing* with his wife. I have se-
lected this couple as an apt example, because they are both persons of good understandings, improved by liberal education ;
they were both possessed of ample fortune,
and came together from mutual attachment ;
but having no children living, and having in
ten years time exhausted all their stock of
conversation, and with it almost all affection,
they never meet but to lament the emptiness
of life, and to reproach each other for the sys-
tem of dissipation which each adopts to banish
painful thoughts.

H 4   THAT

THAT thought is painful, all wife men have lamented; and the wifeſt has confeſſed, that he could find no real ſatisfaction in his prodigious ſhare of underſtanding. All men whoſe ſituation exempts them from mere manual labour, are anxious to diſpel the horrors of reflection; and the thoughts of the moſt virtuous man, without ſome diſſipation or amuſement, call it relaxation, would ſoon become intolerable. Aſk this man why he fiddles? another why he travels? a third why he reads? they will all tell you, that they muſt do ſomething to paſs dull life away; for no man is equal to the dreadful taſk of drawing all his enjoyment from the contemplation of his intellectual powers, or to live a whole winter on his own thoughts, as a bear is ſaid to do by ſucking its own paw.

THE general uſe of *Narcotics* in every country, ſeems to point out that man is not always equal to the pain of thought; and thoſe whom fate has not deſtined to reap the golden wheat with the ſweat of their brows, muſt gather the gaudy poppy that grows mixed amongſt it. Almoſt one half of human life is dedicated to natural ſleep; and of the remaining half, there are few men of

ſprightly

fprightly genius, or intenfe thought, who
have not occafionally facrificed fome part to
artificial infenfibility, either by the ufe of
ftrong liquors, the fumes of tobacco, the excefs of food, or the more dangerous application of even opium itfelf.   -

THERE is a fpecies of *Diffipation*, which as
it appears lefs grofs, fo it is more fafhionable
at prefent: this is *Mufick*; the bewitching influence of fweet founds, draws the attention
with irrefiftible force; and though I can fuppofe that the theory of this Art may be a laborious exercife to the intellectual faculty;
yet mere practical *mufick*, fo far from bur-
thening the thoughts, feems to poffefs the
power rather of draining and purifying them,
while it effectually draws off reflection
from every thing but itfelf. It is not thus
with *painting* or *fculpture*; for an able mafter
will join in the converfation with perfons,
whofe features he is at the time endeavouring to reprefent; but the mufician cannot
fiddle and converfe; even the fimple act of
whiftling denotes, and requires a vacuity of
mind; and thus the clown is aptly defcribed, "whiftling as he went for want of
" thought."

THESE, Sir, are my fentiments on *Diffi-*
pation, and I leave you to extract what

H 5

moral

moral you may pleaſe; but if you are at a loſs, I would hint, that ſince ſome ſort of relaxation is neceſſary to man, *that kind* ſhould be preferred which appears leaſt likely to injure his fortune, or his health; and I am of opinion, that hunting is better than horſe-racing; that hemming a pocket hand-kerchief, or darning an apron, are better than gaming; and that muſick is better than getting drunk; but if you are as tired of reading as I am of writing, you'll agree, that of all ſpecies of Diſſipation, ſleep is the beſt, and ſo wiſhing you a good night, I beg you will believe me, Sir, one of your conſtant readers to kill time.

THEOPHILUS THINKABIT.

N U M B E R   XIX.

___

SIR,

WHEN I tell you how much I have
been adored, how often my charms
have been celebrated in verfe, and my airs
and graces have been fung to mufic; in fhort,
when I introduce myfelf to you as a *wit*, a
beauty, and a *toaft*, I am fure my favours
will be highly prized; efpecially, when you
know that I have been flattered fo long, that
my head is not turned by adulation, and my
experience has ripened all thofe qualities,
which raifed me to the pinnacle of admiration;
for I am not now what I once was, the hair-
brained, giddy, unexperienced hoyden; but

an

an accomplished virgin of the middle age, I think it is somewhere about forty.

From the earliest of my remembrance, my favourite passion was the love of dress; this I inherited from my mother, who once told me that she herself, furnished the Specta-tor with some of his best hints on that im-portant article; as indeed, I myself, have done your predecessor, Mr. *Fitzadam*, in his papers of the World. I invented the treble ruffle and ruffle-cuff, and I was the first woman in the kingdom, who introduced the pinking-iron: but if you would judge both of my person and dress, you will find me represented the most elegant personage in that group of figures, painted by *Boitard*, and engraved by *Patton*, under the title of *Taste a la Mode*, 1745, though I believe the date is wrong. It is therefore with some propriety that *I* may speak of fashions; I, who have been an observer and a follower of them, through such great variety of changes; and it is in this necessary branch of a peri-odical paper, that I mean to offer you my service. But to shew you my *capability* of being a useful correspondent, I shall proceed methodically, (for if I can ever deserve the name of an *old maid*, it must be from my

great

great love of method) and therefore, I shall begin with properly confidering the word *Fashion* itself, and how it has been called at different times.

THERE have been almoft as many words to fignify what is fafhionable, as there have been forts of ftuffs to cover ladies perfons; but fince to be *fafhionable* is *all in all*, fo they have always added that very fignificant word *all*, to every different name. I remember when it was *all the tafte*, to fee a lady cloathed in velvets and brocades; the damafks and water'd tabies were *all the mode*, and a filk fo rich and thick, that it would ftand alone, was *all the go*: fome few years after, luteftrings were invented, and then we goddeffes were dreffed in clouds, for they were *all the thing*; till on a fudden it was *all the rage* to appear in chintz and dimity: thefe, with muflins, tiffany, and gauze, were lately *all the ton*, and would continue to remain fo ftill, but for the enormous price and fcarcity of filk, which I forefee will make filk gowns foon *all the wear*.

IF the materials of which a drefs is made, can have undergone fo many changes in fo fhort a time as I remember; confider, Sir, how infinitely various muft have been the

forms

forms in which thofe gowns were made, from the Sack to the Polonaife, and from the Negligee to the Chemife la Reine, with all the varieties of full-drefs, half-drefs, and un-drefs gowns. I have feen heads moulded into every fhape that whim could invent, or the ingenuity of man could execute : the hair has been taught to ftand up, hang down, ftick out, or twift about in every direction : at one time that it fhould. fmell of mufk, was *all the tafte* ; then to flow free from greafe, in eafy ringlets, was *all the mode* ; then to ftand ftiff and clotted with pomatum, was *all the go* ; and then again combed fmooth, was *all the rage.* Lately, a gauze handkerchief by way of cap, was *all the ton* ; and then to wear nothing at all, was *all the thing* ; but now it is all the fafhion to wear hats and bonnets ; and this laft fafhion does the higheft honour to the fex, as you will yourfelf confefs, when you know whence *this ftile of head-drefs* proceeded. The mafters of ceremony in certain public places of amufement, had impertinently requefted ladies not to ap-pear in HATS, as if *they* were judges of what beft became our fex ; and fome prefumed to exert their authority fo far, as to refufe ad-mittance to a hat or bonnet in a concert-

room,

room, upon which the ladies ingeniously invented the *hat cap*, a fort of a mule betwixt
a hat and a cap, and which fo puzzled thefe
impertinent dictators, that at length they
have fubmitted to leave ladies heads to their
own difcretion, and are ready to acknowledge
them full dreffed, although they fhould come
naked and uncovered.

THERE is one peculiarity in all fafhions, which is whimfical and unac-
countable; and that is, the fudden tran-
fition from one *extreme* to the other. There
feems to be a' fort of fympathy betwixt the
moft diftant parts of the human body. Tops
and bottoms rife and fall together; and what
is worn in one fituation, may be equally becoming in another: thus I have known a
gauze fig-leaf apron worn as a morning cap,
and a diamond ftay-kook converted to a hair-
pin; but of all ftrange changes, that, refpecting cufhions is the oddeft; for in former
times, when cane-backed chairs, and jointed
ftools, were ufed inftead of fophas, the cufhion had an inferior ftation, and helped to
bear the weight of well-dreffed women; but
now it is exalted, and every well-dreffed woman, carries a cufhion on her head.

I MAY perhaps hereafter convince you,
that my obfervations on drefs, have not been

confined

confined to my own fex only; for amongft
my numerous admirers, the moft fafhionably
dreffed, were always the moft encouraged:
I fpeak of beaux a few years back, for the
infipid fops of the prefent day, are fuch fenfe-
lefs idiots, I have given them up, fince they
can prefer the fmiles and gigling of fixteen,
to the more feafoned and experienced beauties
of a middle-aged woman: You, I am fure,
know better, and in this conviction, I remain

Very truly,

Yours,

Tabitha Hasbeen.

There is a part of Mifs Tabitha's letter, which reminds me of an Occafional
Epilogue, fpoken at a private theatre, and
which began thus :———

Fafhion! (whom all obey and who it feems
Delights to fhew her freaks in the extremes)
Fafhion! (dread arbitrefs of heads and tails,
Changing their fhape, as *great* or *fmall* prevails,
From Heidleberg's fly cap to Charlotte bonnet)
Fafhion, is always right, depend upon it.

Of

Of the truth contained in this laft line, I am
fo well convinced, that I fhall always ftudy
to be in the fafhion; and I think it would
not be difficult to prove, that my papers
actually ought to be fo. As the fyllogifm is
the moft correct method of arguing, I will
try to demonftrate this fact, to thofe who
know any thing of logic; thus, *Alteration
is the effence of Variety, and all Fafhion confifts
in Alteration—ergo—Variety muft ever be in
Fafhion. q. e. d.*

Some will perhaps wifh my intelligence,
refpecting thefe alterations, could be furnifh-
ed by a younger correfpondent than Mifs
Tabby; but I confider the communications
of that venerable fpinfter as highly valuable,
for as fafhions come about again in a certain
feries of years, fhe may be fometimes able to
fortell what will be worn next Spring or
Autumn; and fuch intelligence may be of
the higheft confequence to thofe who lay up
cloathes, inftead of giving them to upper
fervants: indeed fhe has fhewn a glimpfe of
this prophetic fpirit in her letter, where fhe
mentions the return of filks; and in her poft-
cript, which I fuppreffed on account of its
length, fhe compares many articles of female
drefs to former times; viz. the prefent *great*

coat

coat to the ancient *Joseph*, and the present high-crowned bonnet, to Mother Shipton's hat. She also talks of the ancient fartingale and petenlair, two harsh-sounding names for things, which she says, once were *all the crack*: the first comes from the Low Dutch Vierdendeel, meaning the hind quarter; and the other, I know not from whence; for she does not say how they were displayed, or on what *extremities* they were used.

I SHALL conclude, with an assurance to my young female readers, that I will never recommend as really the *thing*, any but what is *the pink of the mode*, the *tip-top of the fashion*, the *pinnacle of bon ton*, and the *highest stile of taste*; and thus, whatever *Variety* may produce, I doubt not, my paper will be *all the rage*, *the go*, and *the crack*, as the true means of knowing " which is the way they " wear 'm in."

N U M-

N U M B E R   XX.

The following Letter was fo covered with hair powder, and feemed to have been written in fuch hafte, that I had fome difficulty in making it out.

My dear good old GENTLEMAN,

I AM delighted with you, for promifing to write about the fafhions; for papa makes me read your paper to him, and I am vapoured to death with your long Allegros, or Allegories, as he calls them, though I thank you heartily for the pretty love ftory: but pray, dear Sir, don't let that fufty old maid *bore* us with her treble ruffles; I hardly know what a ruffle was, for my mama cut all

her's

her's up into robbins for me, when I firſt came out in the world laſt winter ; if you want to know what is worn, come to our rout next week, or call on me any morning, and I'll ſhew you my new hat ;—but now I think on't, you muſt come to-morrow, or you can't ſee it with the orange ribbons, for I muſt put on the *roſe fletrie* ribbons, to ſuit my new *barbe de huitre*—I ſhall never be dreſſed in time tho' Winn frizzes quicker than any body—and I doubt you won't be able to make out my letter, for I am writing upon my knee—and the German with a hard name, is waiting below with my new gown—ſo adieu, dear dear little WEATHERCOCKY, and be ſure you write about faſhions.

P. S. An old good for nothing toad to quarrel with our beaux for liking ſixteen better than ſixty—but mind me, and don't mind her—for I ſhall be ſixteen next birth day.

P. S. WINN ſays he's going to powder, ſo I muſt leave off, though I have fifty things to ſay.

P. S. " Oh ! have you ſeen the new
" thing-a-mies that Miſs What's-her name
" brought from Paris ? they ſay there will
" be

" be nothing elfe worn—my pen is fo clogged
" with powder, I can only fay once more
" adieu—and be fure you do as I bid you—
" all the men do exactly as I bid them."

I MUST have been very infenfible not to
obey commands conveyed to me in fo pe-
remptory and lively a manner, and therefore,
refolved to go and procure a pattern of
her new gown, before I difcovered, that
in her hafte, (I fuppofe) my young correfpondent had forgot to add either a name
or date to her letter; I therefore fat me down
in earneft to confider how I might pleafe her,
little thinking that my Speculations on
Fafhion, would prove fo honourable to my fair
country women, as I perceive they will.

HERE let me exult in the reflection, that I
am born to celebrate an æra in Englifh
hiftory, when modefty is arrived at its higheft
pitch; when the extreme delicacy both in our
words and drefs, makes it very difficult to
fpeak of former times without fhocking the
ears (if they have any) of fine Ladies and
Gentlemen. All my predeceffors were continually lamenting the indecency of Ladies in
their time; the SPECTATOR found full employment in pulling down their petticoats, or
pulling

pulling up their tuckers; and the author of the WORLD, speaks of Ladies " *moulting* " their clothes, and shudders lest they should " strip and appear stark naked in the depth of " winter, making both ends meet."

POETS in former ages, celebrated parts of the human body, which must not now be named or hinted at; but without going back to the descriptions in the song of Solomon, we can hardly read a Pope, a Prior, or a Dryden, without wondering at the bold indecencies of their language, and I would seriously recommend that in all future editions of those authors, proper alterations be made, such for instance as this,

On her *white breast* a sparkling cross she wore,
Which Jews might kiss, and Infidels adore.

This passage is now hardly intelligible, unless the whiteness is supposed to allude to the gauze handkerchief, for it could never be supposed that Ladies displayed their breasts; yet from the several epithets of heaving, panting, swelling, &c. which we every where meet with in our best English authors, we must either suppose that there was no decency in those times, or that the Poetic licence empowered these bold gentry to examine what
they

they have so faithfully described. So late as
the year 1770, when I was abroad, it was the
fashion in Germany, for women not only
to display their naked bosoms, but their
gowns were so contrived, that both their
shoulders and elbows were perfectly uncovered; while in France, though women seemed to shew as much, it was impossible to
see their skins, at least to touch them; for
they covered their face and neck with a coat
of paint, so thick, that there could be no in-
delicacy in any quanity of their persons which
they might choose to expose to view : yet they
contrived to reserve a particular spot of pure
natural complexion for great favourites; this
·I discovered by the condefcension of a charming little *Marquise*, who when she found me
obstinate in claiming a salute *a l'Anglois*,
at our parting, she pointed with her fore
finger to a place near the tip of her ear, saying, " tenez mechant diable si'il faut que
" vous me baisez, touchez là;" and I have
since thought that from hence might come the
phrase of " gaining a Lady's ear."

HISTORIANS tell us that the original inha-
'bitants of Britain went naked; but tho' that
was necessary to comply with the fashion
of those times, they covered the whole of
their

their body with paint of such a thickness as
to keep the sexes at a certain distance from
each other's persons; yet the whole shape
and contour of the limbs must have been vi-
sibly exposed; and though they endeavoured
to conceal their earthly bodies, by various re-
presentations of the heavenly bodies painted
on them; yet I think our present notions of
decorum would have been greatly shocked;
for however well the sun and moon, and stars,
might be executed on their bare flesh, I am
afraid they could never be half so elegant
a covering as a bustle or a bishop.

But now let me call up the attention of those
common place moralists, who lament the dege-
neracy of modern times, and the decrease of modesty and virtue. So far from exposing to the
vulgar eye an elbow, a shoulder, or a bosom,
few lovers can boast of having seen their mis-
tress display a throat, an ear, or even a chin;
the arms are covered with a length of sleeve,
unknown to the most prudish of our female
ancestors, and when a fashionable morning
cap is worn, the tip end of the nose, and
centre of the mouth, are all the features that
are visible; and I have no doubt but that the
delicacy of the sex, will at length invent a
covering even for these. But why should I
suggest

fuggeft hints to my fair country women, whofe fafhionable modefty has almoft entirely fhut them out from our view ; they have with wonderful art contrived to become almoft invifible, while they occupy more fpace than ever, and evade our fight, tho' they are three times their natural fize.   To explain this to after-ages, I muft acquaint them that Englifh Ladies in the years 1786 and 87, effected this miraculous difguife, not only by covering, but by adding fuch forms and fhapes to the thing concealed, as 'tis impoffible to believe could ever grow upon a human body.   Lately the Faculty were alarmed at the epidemical fwellings which appeared *behind*, till on examination they were found to proceed from the unnatural ufe of corks; a fafhion fo whimfical and unprecedented, that Sir Afton Leaver thought it right to preferve a fpecimen of thefe pofterior ornaments, in his valuable Mufeum, to fhew pofterity the manner in which corks were fitted to their grand-mothers.   About the fame time, moft enormous protuberances feized all ranks of females in front, which at firft it was feared proceeded from cancerous affections ; but on a clofer examination of thefe formidable tumors, it was difcovered, that there was often *nothing* in 'em ; but that

I

by

by the help of ftarch, wire, and whalebone,
Ladies could raife their bofoms to their
mouths (like cropper pigeons) without pain.
This fafhion would furnifh a powerful argu·
ment for the fuperior difcretion of modern
Belles, if it were neceffary; for who would
hefitate to truft any fecret to a Lady's bofom
where there is room to conceal a lap dog, or
even a lover, if he could be made to fold and
flip into himfelf like a Lady's fliding fan?

Some ill-natured carpers have pretended to
find fault with this fort of bofom *man-trap*
and tell us, that thofe hide moft, who have
really leaft to fhew; if this be fo, it is arran
fwindling, obtaining credit for charms or
falfe pretences; or to fay the leaft of it, 'ti
like the difguifes in French cookery, where
man who chufes a difh by its appearance
may find a fkinny breaft of mutton, where h
expected a delicious tongue and udder.

A few evenings ago, as I paffed throug
the Strand, in my way to tea with the fafhion
able Widow *Jointure*, I was befet by fome c
thofe miferable objects who difgrace the ftreet
of this metropolis, and having extricated my
felf from a groupe almoft as naked as th
Goddeffes on Mount Ida; I was engaged t
a train of thoughts upon the contraft

o

our modeſt women's dreſs, till I reached the
houſe; but when the ſervant opened the par-
lour door, I ſtarted back, ſuppoſing that by
miſtake, he had ſhewn me into the Lady's
dreſſing room, the company being all females,
and moſt of them in their ſhift ſleeves; I
bluſhed, begged pardon, and would have retired, when the fair Widow dragged me
in, and explained the whole myſtery; it ſeems
ſhe and her friends were dreſſed in what they
called *Chemiſe la Reine*, but ſuch is the
extreme delicacy of Engliſh Ladies, that
though 'tis faſhionable to wear a ſhift like
that of the Queen of France, yet in this
country, it is worn over the gowns, and the
Ladies all aſſured me, they had the uſual
quantity of Engliſh linen underneath.   Can
any thing more ſtrongly evince the decency of
the preſent times, that where faſhion makes
it neceſſary to ſhew an under garment, it is
done without the ſmalleſt violation of decorum, by this ingenious mode of making a
ouble ſhift?

THE only people who can complain of
his envelopement of perſon, are Sculptors and
ainters, who conſider *Le Nud*, or repreſent-
ig naked figures, as the higheſt excellence

of their profeſſion ; they can now only ſhew
their ſkill in works of imagination, ſuch
as mermaids, ſyrens, ſphinxes, and the like
monſtrous animals. I would adviſe theſe
Gentlemen to turn their attention to drapery,
ſince they muſt ſoon find full employment in
making handkerchiefs and tuckers to all
our family pictures, to hide the nakedneſs of
thoſe who lived before the introduction of dry
nurſing.

NUM-

N U M B E R XXI.

——————————————

TIME, contrary to the nature of every other poffeffion, is moft neglected by him, who has moft of it upon his hands. Whenever I feel myfelf inclined to be idle and thoughtlefs, my cuftom is, to put on my hat and ftroll through the ftreets juft as accident prompts me ; for there, it is impoffible to be either idle or thoughtlefs, becaufe the objects are in a continued wave of Variety ; and the avoiding cart wheels, close elbows, and um-brella fticks, always provides fufficient employment for both mind and body. I had yefterday juft walked off one of thefe fits, as I found myfelf at the door of a friend, as idle as myfelf, but from whofe leifure I had been often promifed a paper for *Variety* ; I knocked, gave in my name, and the fervant returned with an anfwer, " my mafter is dreffing, Sir, " but begs you will fit down till he can come

" to you, in the mean while he defires to re-
" commend a volume of Lloyd's St. James's
" Magazine, in which he hopes you will find
" fomething new." I fmiled at the idea
of looking for novelty in an old Magazine,
but carelefsly turning over the leaves, I difcovered a M S poem in my friend's hand
writing.

WHETHER like the appetite after exercife,
my mind from having juft fhaken off a fit of
indolence, became more craving and keen in
her exertions, another time muft determine;
at prefent I need but obferve, that the perufal
of the poem gave me confiderable pleafure,
and from a belief that my fatisfaction proceeded rather from its own merit, than
the ftate of my mind at the time, I fhall fub-
join a few extracts from it, with fuch obfervations as occurred to me on its firft perufal.
The idea feems to have been fuggefted by the
almoft total defertion of the Tragic Mufe,
and by remarking the ill fuccefs that has
of late attended the Tragedies of the prefent
day; an event that proves the fluctuating
ftate of fafhion, which, when even founded on
a juft admiration of great powers and fine act-
ing, has not been able to ftand the teft of more
than two or three years. But to our poem:

To

To Jove in Council t'other day,
Sitting (so Heavenly records say)
MELPOMENE in fears complained,
That Comedy alone now reigned;
That mortals felt, she knew not why,
Afraid to see a Hero die.
In verse, that is, for us to prose,
The stage cou'd shew a bloody nose,
Receiv'd with rapture by Mendoze'.
Then she harangu'd with tragic wail,
And told a piteous doleful tale.

How TRIUMPH, who in wanton car,
Had dragg'd the enslaved sons of war,
Was forc'd to lay her carriage down,
And walk on foot to take her crown.

Her torch refusing now to burn,
ALECTO scarce her bread cou'd earn;
Kick'd out from all but good old Drury,
She look'd still more and more the Fury.

How SUICIDE, for want of pelf,
Had rais'd her dagger 'gainst herself.
And POISON in despair, (poor soul!)
Seem'd half inclin'd to taste her bowl.

That MADNESS was so raving grown,
She scarce cou'd call one lock her own;
And that 'twou'd take at least a year,
To grow another head of hair.

I 4   Then

THEN follows a recital of the neglect and mortification suffered by Tragic Authors and Actors; and her speech closes with the enumeration of poor Melpomene's own grievances, which take up many lines, and though all painted with the same justness and strength of colouring, would exceed in detail the limits of our paper. The Author then proceeds:

> All this she urg'd, and much more too;
> The rest the Poet never knew;
> His record only says, the maid
> Great pathos in her cause display'd;
> Adding, " there was an end to merit,
> " And that indeed she cou'd not bear it."
> She cou'd not; no; by all that's good,
> (Far be't from him to think she cou'd.)

AND here let me address the classic reader, who no doubt, in the

Far be't from him to think she cou'd,

must observe a strong resemblance to the famous passage in the sixth book of the Æneid, which whole book is neither more nor less than that most admirable of poetic machines, a *Galanty Shew*, and exhibits a proof that Magic Lanthorns existed so far back as the days

of

of Auguſtus. In that book Virgil paſſes a review of all the Romans of any note, and like a modern Shew-man, who ſhuts the ſcene up with the exhibition of ſome monſter or Monarch of the preſent period, the Poet concludes his ſhew with the ſhade of Marcellus, in compliment to Octavia before whom he rehearſed it. After telling us

Hunc tantum oſtendent terris fata,

he winds up the intereſting climax with that fine apoſtrophe to the ſhade itſelf,

Heu miſerande puer! ſiquâ fata aſpera rumpas,
Tu Marcellus eris.

I HAVE no doubt but our Poet alſo had the

Fungar inani munere

in his mind, and which he conſidered as a friendly tribute due to the feelings of MEL-POMENE; and though his apoſtrophe may not be ſo pathetic as Virgil's, (nor was it neceſſary that it ſhould be ſo) yet we muſt allow it is introduced with equal propriety.

THEN follows a deſcription of the effects which her appeal had on Jupiter:

E'en Jove himſelf in pity lent,
An ear to ev'ry argument;

I 5

With

With face as meek as water gruel,
He chuck'd her chin, and "faith 'twas cruel,"
" 'Twas hard, by Styx, he cried 'twas hard,"
" He pitied ev'ry Tragic Bard ;
" But for herself sweet maid, he thought
" Her case with ev'ry hardship fraught ;
" And if his int'rest cou'd enhance
" Her claim, she'd have his countenance."
He spoke, then stroking smooth his beard,
Desir'd the Gods might be prepar'd:
And summon'd to attend above.
  Subpœnas issued sign'd by Jove,
" Witness ourself upon Olympus,"
And ev'ry Dæmon, God, and Imp was
Serv'd with the order to debate,
Melpomene's unhappy fate.

By custom immemorial, when Poets have
any great design to execute, they are allowed
to feel some diffidence of their being equal to
it. Homer, Virgil, Milton, all address their
Muses under such impressions. Our Author's
design here is to draw a picture of the different
Deities ascending to Olympus, to attend the
trial, and feeling this commendable modesty,
he exclaims,

Oh ! that I'd powers to sing or say,
The wonders of this wond'rous day ! ! !

Thus

Thus in two lines expreffing as much as another could have done in twenty. But having compared the confufion to a *call of the Houfe,* or rather to the thronging together of all the *great men* of a County, to attend a Quarter Seffion, he tells us,

How *Vulcan* on his game leg buftl'd;
And in his hurry *Neptune* huftl'd;
Of all odd fights fure this the oddeft!
Goddefs on God, and God on Goddefs,
Promifcuous mounted on the wing, .
Like onions bunch'd on the fame ftring,
But hold! fome people titter, fee;
Ladies, there's no indecency;
For tho' they rofe one top of t'other,
And *Cupid* flew beneath his mother;
Each Goddefs (mark my words I beg)
Wore Opera Draw'rs to hide her leg.

THE above paffage is perfectly natural. The Poet, trembling more for the uncleannefs of other men's imaginations, than his own, halts under the alarm, left fome wicked wit fhould fancy he had difcovered that *Minerva's* ancles were rather thicker than her underftanding; or that *Pfyche,* who before her marriage with *Cupid,* was the neateft creature in the world, had fince become fo great a flattern as to garter below knee, and tie up her

I 6   ftockings

ftockings with a piece of packthread, or
a dirty ribbon. After defcribing the perfons
and dreffes of many of the celeftials, the poem
fays,

> But fure our Poet need not ftoop,
> To take the fize of ev'ry hoop;
> Whether the dames wore ftays or jumps
> Reduc'd their bofoms and their rumps.
> If *Juno fported* a fky blue,
> Or pink, or *buff*, or fomething new;
> It matters not, for thro' this fport,
> We never fhall get into Court:
> Suppofe ourfelves then ftanders by,
> Viewing this Jury of the fky;
> Suppofe each God being fworn and feated,
> Mr. Chief Juftice *Jove* has greeted;
> The briefs deliver'd, Counfel feed,
> The caufe call'd on, they thus proceed.

THEN follow the arguments of the Plead-
ers, examination of Witneffes, *Jove's* fum-
ming up of the Evidence, and at length the
decifion of the Gods, viz. That as paffions were given to mankind to be the fource
of good or evil, and as the experience of
centuries had not impeached the wifdom of
fuch a fyftem, it was bad precedent to inter-
rupt its operation till fome inconvenience

made

made it neceſſary to do ſo; that is, in plain Engliſh, and to uſe a very vulgar proverb, no more than ſaying, " let every man follow his " noſe, and go to the devil his own way;" a deciſion particularly honourable to the liberty of the ſoil we breath in, where each man picks out and purſues that path which ſeems the neareſt to him, and either cuts his throat or blows his brains out, as Fear or Fancy may direct. Tho' however the decree is wiſdom, it is a hardſhip on poor *Melpomene*, whom as the ruined Heroine of his poem, the Author thus compaſſionates:

> But oh! let pity heave a ſigh,
> And drop her tear to miſery;
> Juſtice, ſhe owns, ſhou'd act with vigour,
> But even Juſtice may be rigour:
> And while the head approves the law,
> The heart wou'd gladly find a flaw.

AFTER thus lamenting the fate of *Melpomene*, and that there ſhould not be any appeal from the decrees of Jove in Council, (though if he has any regard for the Muſe, he would never wiſh to put her into *Equity*) the manuſcript diſplays the triumph of Comedy at the defeat of her ſiſter, and that Miſs *Thalia*, notwithſtanding the Court has ſat ſo long, prepares

pares to announce her victory to the mad-headed fons of earth that very night.

> At twelve, I think, yes twelve; I'm right :
> (For *Mufes* vifit in the night)
> And tho' fome folk may cry the trade is
> A little ftrange for modeft Ladies)
> Yet think what mortal dare refufe
> Admittance to a knocking *Mufe?*
> Knowing her rap, pray where's the fin,
> To rife and let the Goddefs in?

THALIA is now on the pinion for our little world in the middle of the night; and this opens a fine field for the defcription of flambeaux and other wonders, by which her defcent was marked; and the account is concluded by a beautiful profopopeia, in which he perfonifies *Senfibility*, *Wit*, and *Humour*, and by attributing to their perfons the refpective features that diftinguifh thefe qualities of the mind, has given us a fine piece of canvas, the painting of which makes us feel an intereft for *Comedy*, who is fo charmingly attended.

> ———Here DANCE and SONG,
> By Tendrils from a Vine-Twig link'd
> With anticks at each other wink'd;
> Led on by HARMONY's full band,
> The *Mufe* appear'd; on her right hand
>
> Lean'd

Lean'd Sensibility, fweet youth;
And Wit that fcorn'd the low untruth,
Good nature written in his face,
He fpoke with fuch bewitching grace,
That tho' his words were keen ftrong fenfe,
Not one of them cou'd give offence;
On her left hand, in frolic mood,
Holding his fides, broad Humour ftood;
Who for his life cou'd never weep,
But laugh'd and giggl'd in his fleep.

I cannot fuffer the reader to go on without here requefting, that he will again perufe
this charming defcription of the Attendants
of *Comedy*, and if he is not pleafed with it
he may conclude that he has no tafte for poetry.

The Author then defcribes the effect this
decree had on various Tragic Writers; but
I fhall felect only the following lines, which
I hope are written prophetically:

The far heard found reach'd *Jephfon*'s ears,
Jephfon with *Julia* fat in tears,
His arm thrown fondly round her waift,
Sad fatire on the public tafte}
With woe paft utterance elate,
They fat in filent forrow's ftate.
As Wit for them had loft its zeft,
Each turn'd and wept in t'other's breaft.

In Irish emphasis he swore,
Never to soil his paper more.
Vows, made 'neath *Passion*'s influence,
Against all rule of common sense,
Honour bids break; we praise with pride,
The man who owns that nobler guide,
Propriety, with bold contrition,
Who spurns the ignoble superstition
Of a weak oath; weak only when
Our hand subscribes with folly's pen,
Jephson but swore to shew us how,
Merit shou'd break a rash made vow.

THE Poem now concludes with telling us
that the triumph of Comedy was very short, for
sick of the sorry stuff she now met with, and
having no hopes from either *Murphy* or *Sheri-
dan*, who had each burnt their pens, the
Muse *Thalia* returned to Olympus in almost as
great distress as her sister, declaring that the
Genius of Nonsense had by the help of *Farce* and
Pantomime, taken full possession of the stage,
and the Poem finishes with these lines:

Nor, Reader, shoud'st thou hence infer
On either *Muse*'s fame, a slur;
Our taste, and not *their* merit's chang'd;
(The world 'neath folly's banner rang'd)

Our

Our Authors with corrupted thirst,
Now struggle who shall be the first
To paint the ablest Scaramouch :
Nor will *the* Poet's foresight vouch,
The Actor's *laurel* may not soon .
Be *grafted* on the best Buffoon ;
And Wit, and Sense, each yield his place,
To the wild nonsense, odd grimace,
Of *Edwin's* song, and *Edwin's* face.

NUMBER XXII.

S I R,

I LABOUR under a species of diftrefs, which I fear will at length drive me utterly from that fociety, in which I am moft ambitious to appear; but I will give you a fhort fketch of my origin and prefent fituation, by which you will be enabled to judge of my difficulties.

My Father was a farmer of no great property, and with no other learning than what he had acquired at a charity-fchool; but my mother being dead, and I an only child, he determined to give me that advantage, which he fancied would have made him happy, viz. a learned education.—I was fent to a coun-

try

try grammar-fchool, and from thence to the University, with a view of qualifying for holy orders. Here, having but fmall allowance from my father, and being naturally of a timid and bafhful difpofition, I had no opportunity of rubbing off that native awkwardnefs, which is the fatal caufe of all my unhappinefs, and which I now begin to fear can never be amended. You muft know, that in my perfon I am tall and. thin, with a fair complexion, and light flaxen hair; but of fuch extreme fufceptibility of fhame, that on the fmalleft fubjeÉt of confufion, my blood all rufhes into my cheeks, and I appear a perfeÉt full-blown rofe. The confcioufnefs of this unhappy failing, made me avoid fociety, and I became enamoured of a college life; particularly when I refleÉted, that the uncouth manners of my father's family, were little calculated to improve my outward conduÉt; I therefore, had refolved on living at the Univerfity and taking pupils, when two unexpeÉted events greatly altered the pofture of my affairs, viz. my father's death, and the arrival of an uncle from the Indies.

This uncle I had very rarely heard my father mention, and it was generally. believed that he was long fince dead, when he arrived in. England

England only a week too late to close his brother's eyes. I am aſhamed to confeſs, what I
believe has been often experienced by thoſe,
whoſe education has been better than their
parents, that my poor father's ignorance, and
vulgar language, had often made me bluſh to
think I was his ſon; and at his death I was
not inconſolable for the loſs of *that*, which
I was not unfrequently aſhamed to own. My
uncle was but little affected, for he had been
ſeparated from his brother more than thirty
years, and in that time he had acquired a
fortune which he uſed to brag, would make
a Nabob happy; in ſhort, he had brought
over with him the enormous ſum of thirty
thouſand pounds, and upon this he built his
hopes of never-ending happineſs. While he
was planning ſchemes of greatneſs and delight, whether the change of climate might
affect him, or what other cauſe I know not,
but he was ſnatched from all his dreams of
joy by a ſhort illneſs, of which he died, leaving me heir to all his property. And now,
Sir, behold me at the age of twenty-five, well
ſtocked with Latin, Greek, and Mathematics, poſſeſſed of an ample fortune, but
ſo awkard and unverſed in every gentleman-
like

like accomplishment, that I am pointed at by all who fee me, as the *wealthy learned clown.*

I HAVE lately purchafed an eftate in the country, which abounds in (what is called) a fafhionable neighbourhood; and when you reflect on my parentage and uncouth manner, you will hardly think how much my company is courted by the furrounding families, (efpecially by thofe who have marriageable daughters): From thefe gentlemen I have received familiar calls, and the moft preffing invitations, and though I wifhed to accept their offered friendfhip, I have repeatedly excufed myfelf under the pretence of not being quite fettled; for the truth is, that when I have rode or walked, with full intention to return their feveral vifits, my heart has failed me as I approached their gates, and I have frequently returned homeward, refolving to try again to-morrow.

HOWEVER, I at length determined to conquer my timidity, and three days ago, accepted of an invitation to dine this day with one, whofe open eafy manner, left me no room to doubt a cordial welcome. Sir THOMAS FRIENDLY, who lives about two miles diftant, is a baronet, with about two thoufand pounds a year eftate, joining to that I

purchafed;

purchafed; he has two fons, and five daughters, all grown up, and living with their
mother and a maiden fifter of Sir Thomas's,
at *Friendly-Hall*, dependant on their father.
Confcious of my unpolifhed gait, I have for
fome time paft, taken private leffons of a *Pro-
feffor*, who teaches " grown gentlemen to
" dance;" and though I at firft found wonderous difficulty in the art he taught, my
knowledge of the mathematics was of prodigious ufe, in teaching me the equilibrium
of my body, and the due adjuftment of
the centre of gravity to the five pofiti-
ons. Having now acquired the art of walking without tottering, and learned to make
a bow, I boldly ventured to obey the baronet's invitation to a family dinner, not doubting but my new acquirements would enable
me to fee the ladies with tolerable intrepidity :
but alas ! how vain are all the hopes of
theory, when unfupported by habitual *practice*.
As I approached the houfe, a dinner bell alarmed my fears, left I had fpoiled the dinner
by want of punctuality ; impreffed with this
idea, I blufhed the deepeft crimfon, as my
name was repeatedly announced by the feveral
livery fervants, who ufhered me into the
library, hardly knowing what or whom I

faw ;

saw ; at my first entrance, I summoned all my
fortitude, and made my new-learned bow to
Lady FRIENDLY, but unfortunately in bringing back my left foot to the third position, I
trod upon the gouty toe of poor Sir THOMAS,
who had followed close at my heels, to be the
Nomenclator of the family. The confusion
this occasioned in *me*, is hardly to be conceived, since none but bashful men *can* judge of
my distress, and of that description, the number
I believe is very small. The Baronet's polite-
ness by degrees dissipated my concern, and I was
astonished to see how far good breeding could
enable him to suppress his feelings, and to
appear with perfect ease, after so painful an
accident.

THE cheerfulness of her Ladyship, and the
familiar chat of the young ladies, insensibly
led me to throw off my reserve and sheepish-
ness, till at length I ventured to join in conversation, and even to start fresh subjects.
The library being richly furnished with books
in elegant bindings, I conceived Sir THO-
MAS to be a man of literature, and ventured
to give my opinion concerning the several
editions of the Greek classics, in which
the Baronet's opinion exactly coincided with
my own. To this subject I was led, by
observing an edition of *Xenophon* in sixteen

volumes,

volumes, which (as I had never before heard of such a thing) greatly excited my curiosity, and I rose up to examine what it could be: Sir THOMAS saw what I was about, and (as I suppose) willing to save me trouble, rose to take down the book, which made me more eager to prevent him, and hastily laying my hand on the first volume, I pulled it forcibly; but lo! instead of books, a board, which by leather and gilding had been made to look like sixteen volumes, came tumbling down and unluckily pitched upon a Wedgwood ink-stand on the table under it. In vain did Sir THOMAS assure me, there was no harm; I saw the ink streaming from an inlaid table on the Turkey carpet, and scarce knowing what I did, attempted to stop its progress with my cambrick handkerchief. In the height of this confusion, we were informed that dinner was served up, and I with joy perceived that the bell, which at first had so alarmed my fears, was only the half-hour dinner-bell.

IN walking through the hall, and suite of apartments to the dining-room, I had time to collect my scattered senses, and was desired to take my seat betwixt Lady FRIENDLY and her eldest daughter at the table. Since the fall of the wooden *Xenophon*, my face had been
continually

continually burning like a firebrand, and I
was juſt beginning to recover myſelf, and to
feel comfortably cool, when an unlooked for
accident, rekindled all my heat and bluſhes,
Having ſet my plate of ſoup too near the
edge of the table, in bowing to Miſs DINAH,
who politely complimented the pattern of my
waiſtcoat, I tumbled the whole ſcalding contents into my lap. In ſpite of an immediate
ſupply of napkins to wipe the ſurface of my
cloaths, my black ſilk breeches were not ſtout
enough to ſave me from the painful effects of
this ſudden fomentation, and for ſome minutes, my legs and thighs ſeemed ſtewing in a
boiling cauldron ; but recollecting how Sir
THOMAS had diſguiſed his torture, when I
trod upon his toe, I firmly bore my pain in
ſilence, and ſat with my lower extremities
parboiled, amidſt the ſtifled giggling of the
ladies and the ſervants.

I WILL not relate the ſeveral blunders
which I made during the firſt courſe, or the
diſtreſs occaſioned by my being deſired to carve
a fowl, or help to various diſhes that ſtood
near me, ſpilling a ſauce-boat, and knocking
down a ſalt-ſeller ; rather let me haſten to the
ſecond courſe, " where freſh diſaſters over-
" whelmed me quite."

K

I HAD

I HAD a piece of rich sweet pudding on my fork, when Miss LOUISA FRIENDLY begged to trouble me for a pigeon, that stood near me; in my haste, scarce knowing what I did, I whipped the pudding into my mouth, hot as a burning coal; it was impossible to conceal my agony, my eyes were starting from their sockets. At last, in spite of shame and resolution, I was obliged to drop the cause of torment on my plate. Sir THOMAS and the Ladies all compassionated my misfortune, and each advised a different application; one recommended oil, another water, but all agreed that wine was best for drawing out the fire; and a glass of sherry was brought me from the sideboard, which I snatched up with eagerness : but, oh! how shall I tell the sequel? whether the butler by accident mistook, or purposely designed to drive me mad, he gave me the strongest brandy, with which I filled my mouth, already flea'd and blistered; totally unused to every kind of ardent spirits, with my tongue, throat, and palate, as raw as beef, what could I do? I could not swallow, and clapping my hands upon my mouth, the cursed liquor squirted through my nose and fingers like a fountain, over all the dishes; and I was crushed by bursts of

laughter

daughter from all quarters. In vain did Sir Thomas reprimand the servants, and Lady Friendly chide her daughters; for the measure of my shame and their diversion was not yet compleat. To relieve me from the intolerable state of perspiration, which this accident had caused, without considering what I did, I wiped my face with that ill-fated handkerchief, which was still wet from the consequences of the fall of *Xenophon*, and covered all my features with streaks of ink in every direction. The Baronet himself could not support this shock, but joined his Lady in the general laugh; while I sprung from the table in despair, rushed out of the house, and ran home in an agony of confusion and disgrace, which the most poignant sense of guilt could not have excited.

Thus, without having deviated from the path of moral rectitude, I am suffering torments like a " goblin damn'd." The lower half of me has been almost boiled, my tongue and mouth grill'd, and I bear the mark of Cain upon my forehead; yet these are but trifling considerations, to the everlasting shame which I must feel, whenever this adventure shall be mentioned; perhaps

K 2

by

by your affistance, when my neighbours know how much I *feel* on the occafion, they will fpare a *bashful man*, and (as I am juft informed my poultice is ready) I truft you will excufe the hafte in which I fubfcribe myfelf,

Yours, &c.

MONGRELL MORELL.

N U M B E R XXIII.

IF we take a view of human life, and consider the various employments and pursuits of all Ranks in Society, how busily
each is engaged to circumvent his neighbour, or to guard against the like attempts
on himself; we shall be apt to conclude, that
the *chief employment* of life is to *cheat* others,
or to prevent being *cheated* ourselves.   This
will appear a harsh declaration to those who
fancy themselves honest, because they have
never considered the full extent and meaning
of the odious word *cheating:* but I fear it
would not be difficult to prove, that few individuals have been totally and at all times
free, from something very near akin to this
universal practice. The GENTLEMAN of great
landed property, and strict honour towards

K 3

his

his equals, if he permit his fteward to lett his land for more than it is fairly worth, may be faid to cheat his tenant of the juft reward of induftry and labour; and fhould his tradefmens' bills be deferred for debts of honour, he cheats *them* of the intereft of their money. TRADE exifts only by what the *gentleman* would call difhonourable cheating; for if a man of landed property, refiding in the country, were to defire another who was going to London, to buy any article for him; and if he were afterwards to difcover that his friend had charged him a greater price than he had actually paid for it, the perfon who had by fuch difhonourable means obtained advantage, would be excern'd as the meaneft *cheat:* but not fo the *Merchant* or the *Shop-keeper*; it is his bufinefs to buy every article in which he deals, at the loweft price; and to fell it with as much advance as poffible: if he could fo fecretly conduct his bargain, that the prime coft could never be difcovered, his confcience would never accufe him of difhonourable *cheating*, for vending the commodity at any rate of profit; and the fole reftriction by which he is confined, is the competition of the neighbouring tradefmen. The *Manufacturer* has a better claim to exhorbi-

tant

tant advantage, as a reward for invention, ingenuity, and manual labour. The *Merchant* dedicates his *time* indeed; but it is often to mix, confound, perhaps adulterate the various commodities which he imports; and what is this but *cheating?* The *Shopkeeper* difplays his wares in the moft tempting fhapes, and attracts the eye with fuperficial excellence, hiding with watchful caution every blemifh. The fubtle *Silk Mercer* darkens the light of Heaven, to cheat you in the finenefs of his ftuffs; and the knowing *Grocer* artfully fets off his dingy fugar, by placing it on paper of a browner hue. All this they tell you is not cheating, becaufe their neighbours do the fame, and it is their bufinefs. With the fame excufe the *Lawyer* pleads a caufe which he knows ought not to be decided in his favour, and cheats the client of a fee. The refiding *Vicar* reluctantly obeys the call to private acts of devotion, and fpends his breath one hour in a week to explain doctrines which he neither comprehends nor credits; or to deliver precepts for moral conduct, which he finds himfelf unable to obey; denouncing vengeance againft fraud and cheating; yet he takes for this poor nugatory fervice, the utmoft farthing which the

K 4

law

law allows ; but if he chance to be of higher rank, perhaps a dignitary of the church, he sends a deputy with scanty salary to perform these duties for which he cheats the industrious peasant of one full tenth of all his crops, improved and raised by anxious labour and fatigue : but it is not *cheating* ; for custom has determined that a wealthy Rector is to have the tythes for doing nothing !   The *Beggar cheats* by exciting pity, with false rags, and a dissembled tale of woe.   The *Beauty cheats* by every curl which nature has denied her person, she cheats with artificial head, and heels, and tail.

I COULD adduce a thousand instances to prove, how every rank and every profession employ their time in *cheating* others ; but I must shew that it is not less urgently employed in counteracting the same intentions of others towards them.   In our conduct towards our *superiors*, if we have occasion to solicit any favour, we must beware lest specious promises cheat us into hopes which cannot be accomplished ; for a flat refusal is uncourteous; yet all cannot expect to be obliged, or served.   Amongst our *equals*, if we form intimate connections, we must be cautious, lest advantage be taken of our friendship, and

our

our open heart be cheated by an ill-deserved confidence; for however illiberal is the maxim, I fear it has been too often confirmed by experience of ingratitude, "that " we should trust a friend with cautious pru- " dence, lest he may become an enemy." As to our *inferiors* and *dependants*, every bolt and bar which defend the outside of our dwellings, and every lock and key with which the inside of a house is furnished, are arguments how much we dread the general propensity, to cheat, rob, and plunder us.

I WAS led to this train of thought, by receiving the following letter from a friend, with whom I have been long acquainted:

" My Dear Wat,

. " YOU will be vexed, if not suprized to " hear, that I am unhappy from a cause " which you long since predicted. In short " I am ruined by the acquisition of fortune. " You have been a witness to the several " stages of my life: you knew me when at " college; and you approved my marriage, " on leaving it, with a woman twelve years " older than myself; whose only qualifica- " tions were, a person not disagreeable, an

ardent

" ardent love for me; and a fortune equal
" to my own, with habits of œconomy to
" make the moſt of it. You know how we
" lived together for nearly ten years in com-
" fortable affluence, without children, and
" I may ſay, almoſt without care; the only
" ſource of diſquiet I ever experienced, pro-
" ceeded from my poor wife's continual oſ-
" tentation of vigilance, and good houſewife-
" ry; ſometimes ſhe would diſturb a pleaſing
" train of thought, by producing odd rem-
" nants of linen for the family, which ſhe
" had bought at half their intrinſic value;
" at other times I was ſummoned to attend
" the unpacking a prodigious cheſt of mer-
" chandize, which had been laid in from
" London at the wholeſale price, becauſe
" the village ſhopkeeper would add a far-
" thing in the pound to every article. At
" breakfaſt I was told of new invented traps
" for catching mice, and was convinced of
" their effect, by having the poor ſtinking
" captives brought in with the bread and
" butter. The comfort of my dinner was
" deſtroyed by comments on the price of
" every diſh; the abatement on a herring,
" or a mackarel; and the exact ſaving of a
" leg of pork, or a ſpring chicken, by breed-
" ing

" ing it ourfelves. At fupper, I was to fit in
" judgment on fome mifcreant fervant who
" had been goffiping too long ; perhaps
" the gardener had fold a cabbage, or the
" cook forgot to fift the cinders clofe ; and a
" large coal was then produced in evidence,
" that had been taken from a neighbouring
" dunghill. Thus my days paffed amidft
" conftant lamentations of my wife, that all
" the world combined to *cheat* us : yet I
" lived with credit and efteem amongft my
" neighbours upon five hundred pounds *per*
" *annum* ; and vied in fplendor and domef-
" tic comforts with thofe who I was told
" were fpending twice my income.

" My union with poor Nelly had rather
" been a match of prudence than of ftrong
" attachment, at leaft on my fide ; (for I be-
" lieve the old Girl loved me almoft as well
" as fhe did houfewifery) but by ftanding
" half naked at the window, to watch the
" maids one wafhing morning, fhe caught a
" cold, which foon became a putrid fever,
" and I loft my buftling houfekeeper after
" only three days illnefs. You know how
" foon I recovered this lofs ; and that before
" twelve months expired, I married the ac-
" complifhed Widow Eafy, with a jointure
" of five hundred pounds *per annum*. We

K 6   have

" have now lived together only feven years ;
" and in that fhort time I find myfelf in-
" volved in difficulties which I cannot com-
" prehend. I am in actual want of ready
" money : you know my own eftate is en-
" tailed on my hopeful nephew ; but what
" furprifes me, is this : I have an income
" now of a THOUSAND pounds *per annum;*
" my appearance is the fame as when I fpent
" five hundred only. I live in the fame
" houfe, keep the fame fervants (except a few
" occafional helpers); have the fame number
" of horfes (except my wife's gray mare) and
" yet I am always poor. They tell me I am
" *cheated* by my fervants, and my tradefmen ;
" but that can never make the difference.
" What fignifies a few fhillings in a bill, or
" a farthing in a pound weight ? for fuch
" trifles I can never fubmit to the tedious
" tafk of cafting their accounts, or cheapen-
" ing their articles ; yet what am I to do ?
" I cannot live upon my prefent income,
" and it is impoffible to retrench or fave a
" hundred pounds. Come quickly to my
" affiftance, and advife me. Meanwhile,
" believe,

Your's, &c.

CHARLES CARELESS."

N U M B.

N U M B E R XXIV.

Dear Sir,

SINCE you are obliged to me for the publication of your papers, I think I have a claim on you to hear my complaints with patience, though you may not be able to redrefs my grievances. I am one of the feven children of the week, by our old Father TIME ; but being the youngeft, have infen-fibly become the worft ufed in the family ; and this cruel treatment is the lefs tolerable to me, from the " remembrance of better " days," and the confcioufnefs of undeferved neglect ; for till within about feventeen or eighteen centuries, I was exalted above all my other fifters. 'Twas then that I enjoyed

thofe

thofe honours which are now beftowed on another; 'twas then, mankind looked up to me with that veneration and refpect which they have now transferred entirely to my eldeft fifter; my hours like her's, were dedicated to reft, and ferious meditation; but now I'm treated as the drudge, and out-caft of my family, as one condemned to finifh all the tafks of labour in which the other daughters of the week have been employed. But let me give a brief defcription how I am received, and treated by the feveral ranks of people in this kingdom.

THE *Manufacturers* or daily *Labourers* employ my mornings with double induftry, that they may compleat the work begun, and receive the reward of their fix days labour, which is oftener paid them in my prefence than in that of any of my fifters; and which they are very apt to lavifh in idlenefs, and drunken folace, with our eldeft fifter, of whofe ufurpation I complain: with thefe people I am generally fo dirty and neglected, that I am often loathfome to myfelf and others, fince no mechanic ever deigns to treat me with clean linnen, and fome not even with clean face or hands: while all their finery as well as neatnefs is referved to

welcome

welcome my fifter, whofe vifits conftantly fucceed at my departure. Yet it is not by drefs alone that fhe is complimented at my expence, but fhe is always better entertained; fhe is regaled with meat, and ale for dinner, while I am hardly allowed mere bread and cheefe. Nay, even in very reputable families, I am obliged to fubmit to cold meat, or difhes hafhed and warmed again ; becaufe, forfooth ! they muft make ends meet whenever I look in upon them. This leads me to relate my treatment in the clafs next above the mere mechanic ; the *petty fhopkeeper* is oftentimes obliged to me, for more bufinefs than to all my other money-getting fifters put together; for as to fifter SUNDAY (as I before obferved) fhe is above attending to any means of getting money, unlefs upon a vifit to the very rich and fafhionable, where fhe condefcends to play a game at cards, to the great fcandal of the inferior neighbours. The petty fhopkeeper, notwithftanding all his obligation, longs for my departure, yet often dedicates an hour or two extraordinary to me by candle-light, that he may be better able to enjoy my fifter's company, by the profits of my protracted occupation; and while I am doomed to cheat and buftle in the city,

he

he waftes the produce of my thrift in indolence and quiet with my fifter in the country.

FROM the mere drudges of a retail trade,
let us go one ftep higher, to thofe who have
been long enough in bufinefs, to leave it
fometimes to a trufty fervant ; it is here I am
made the harbinger of pleafures for my fifter.
For this purpofe I am often hurried from a
fhabby dinner, and wedged into a one-horfe
chaife with the trader's greafy wife, and as
many dirty brats as the chaife will hold, or
crammed into the filthy corner of a ftage, and
whirled into the country, that the family
may be enabled to give a hearty welcome to
my fifter, but while they drefs themfelves in
their beft apparel to appear with her, they
fay, " that any thing is good enough for
" me."

THE rich and great, are thofe that ufe me
beft, for they make no diftinction betwixt
me and any of my fifters ; and though they
do not fhew me any marks of attention or
refpect, yet they never fhock my feelings
by diftinguifhed partialities to my fifter SUN-
DAY ; fo far from it, that her vifits often appear dull, and the fafhionable world look on
her as a fit companion only to the lower orders of mankind ; for what advantage can
thofe

thofe who never *labour*, derive from her, whofe only virtue is to beftow *reft from labour?* Indeed, with thefe exalted members of fociety, it often happens, that all the SEVEN DAUGHTERS of the WEEK have paffed in turns before them, without the fmalleft notice by which they could diftinguifh one of us from an other; and while the induftrious world, receives the call of each of us by fun-rife, the Rich and Great, deny us all admittance till 'tis almoft noon.

THERE is one fect of men who ftill retain for *me* that veneration which all Europe have agreed to fhew my fifter; but their filthy finery, and taudry naftinefs, difguft me fo much, that I feel little honoured by the no-.tice of this cheating, circumcifed people.

To Schoolboys I am always welcome; for I generally bring them half a holiday: but ftill I muft complain of dirty ufage; for the little urchins claim a priviledge of being never clean at my arrival; becaufe they know before I leave them, they muft undergo a thorough cleaning to receive my fifter.

CONSIDER, Sir, how mortifying to me muft be this confideration; yet I have fome flender hope, that things may come about again; for my fifter is of late become fo fanc-

tified

tified and methodiftical, and fome pious and
reforming Juftices have taken her fo cordially
under their fanatical protection, that fhe is
become abominably ftupid to the induftrious
multitude who make our fifters work; and
for this reafon it is not unufual for me to become partaker of thofe joys which were intended for my eldeft fifter; and I am called
forth to witnefs games of fkittles, cricket,
bowls, and trap-ball, which my fifter is not
allowed to fee. Yet thefe amufements give
me pain, fince I am aware that five days labour can but ill fupply the neceffary wants
of *Saturday* and *Sunday*; and as the latter can
never now be brought to work like one of us,
the families of thofe who wifh to fport with
me, becaufe my fifter's fullen temper forbids
the like with her, muft foon be ruined.

I KNOW not what I ought to afk or wifh
of you, but fince you have fhewn fome
partiality to me, I hope you will confider
my complaint, and not fuffer me to become
the filthieft, and moft contemptible amongft
my family. Though I can never hope to be
exalted to thofe honours which my eldeft
fifter has fo long ufurped, I truft you will
recommend an univerfal cleanlinefs; and tell
the world that they ought never to retire to
reft,

reſt, when I have viſited them, without ablution from the dirt of the week ; requeſt of thoſe with whom I paſs my day in drudgery and filth, that they would make me comfortable before we part ; and charge them never to defer this weekly taſk, till it be too late to celebrate with my ſiſter, the public acts of gratitude and praiſe, to which it is her duty to excite mankind.   And ſo, my deareſt Sir, till we meet again, believe me

Yours,

For as long as you pleaſe,

Saturday.

***

SIR,

WE the Underwritten, having by accident ſeen our Siſter's letter, deſire, that (ſhould you think proper to publiſh her complaints) you will alſo inſert our opinion of her.   She is an idle dirty huſſey ; and though ſhe is occaſionally employed to finiſh the work which ſome of us begin, ſhe is hardly ever known

known to set about a serious job herself; but
always makes excuse, by saying, " that it is
" too late to make a bad week's work a good
" one." For this reason, and being the
youngest daughter, she is generally made to
do the work of the family, and is very
properly employed to get the house in order,
to receive our eldest sister, who ought never
to appear like one of us. As to her complaint
of this sister's usurpation, we confess that the
youngest once enjoyed the honours, now bestowed by Christians, on the eldest; but with
this she ought to acquiesce, and not associate
with this stubborn race, who refused to credit
the authority which declared, that the first
should be last, and the last first. We remain

Yours,

As you use us,

Monday,
Tuesday,
Wednesday,
Thursday, and
Friday.

NUM-

" 'Tis hard to fay if greater want of fkill
" Appears in *writing*, or in *judging* ill;
" But, of the two, leaft dangerous is th' offence
" To tire our patience, than miflead our fenfe.
                                        POPE.

IT cannot be doubted that the underftanding, and virtue, the fafety, and happinefs,
of thofe branches of Society which are raifed
above the neceffity of mechanic toil, depend
much upon the early impreffions they receive
from books which captivate the imagination,
and intereft the heart. Confequently a writer
is much their foe, who feeks to throw contempt upon any work which is eminently calculated to infpire delicacy, and difcretion of
conduct, purity of morals, tendernefs, gene-
                                        rofity,

rofity, and piety of heart,—while he recommends another compofition, poffeffing allure-
ment, too well calculated to make it recommend *itfelf*; but which has a demonftrable
tendency to encourage libertinifm in our
young men; and, in our young women, an
infatuated propenfity to beftow their affections, and even efteem upon men of profligate
habits.

THAT an author capable of writing agree-
ably upon many fubjects, who muft have obferved with what difficulty vicious habits,
contracted in early life, are laid afide as it ad-
vances; and that *continued*, how fatal they
prove to domeftic comfort, that a man who is
himfelf a father, fhould avow fuch a preference, and employ his oratory, and aim at
wit in its defence, may well awaken the
wonder and difdain of thinking minds.

A PAPER in Mr. Cumberland's Obferver,
on the fubject of Novels, fuggefted thefe re-
flections. It points out, in that large range
of fafhionable reading, which are the paths
to be *interdicted*, and which *chofen* for young
people by their Parents, and Guardians. From
the praife which its author lavifhes upon
Fielding's Tom Jones, and from his affected
contempt of the *Clariffa of Richardfon*, he
feems

feems to recommend the former to our youth
as forcibly, by implication, as he reprobates
the latter, in direct and pofitive terms. Men
eminent for piety, wifdom, and virtue, have
recommended Richardfon's Clariffa from the
pulpit; a work which Dr. Johnfon, (fo generally unwilling to praife) has been often
heard to pronounce, " not only the firft *novel*,
" but perhaps the firft *work* in our language,
" fplendid in point of genius, and calculated
" to promote the deareft interefts of religion
" and virtue."

THOSE who have ability to perceive the
riches of that work in every varied excellence
of beautiful compofition, will not be infenfible to the merit of the *Tom Jones*, as a fafcinating performance, whofe fituations are interefting, whofe characters difplay the hand
of a mafter, whofe humour is pointed and natural, whofe ftyle is eafy, and to whofe
powers of engaging, the pathetic graces have
not been wanting.

BUT while they acknowledge all thefe
agreeable properties, they will feel it amongft
the moft ftriking inftances of human abfurdity, that a ferious writer fhould recommend it
to the libraries of the rifing generation by
unqualified praife, while he condemns the

Clariffa

Clariffa as a ridiculous romance, inimical to good fenfe, difcretion, and morality.

A LADY of wit and fpirit has been heard to declare, that fhe was once compleatly filenced by a very ftupid perfonage, in the midft of a declamation, and encircled by a large party of ladies and gentlemen. She was haranguing upon the preference fhe fhould feel of Tom Jones, to Sir Charles Grandifon, as a brother, a friend, a lover, or an hufband. The *filly* gentlewoman, in the meer defire of prating, and perfectly uncon-fcious of the power of what fhe was going to utter, interrupted the Lady Orator with, " Ladies and gentlemen, *I* am reading Tom " Jones, but I have not finifhed it. I have " juft left him in bed with another man's " wife."

PERHAPS it is not impoffible, though very uncommon, that bravery, ingenuoufnefs, compaffion, and generofity, fhould exift in the mind of a young man, who is indifcrimi-nately licentious refpecting women ; but it is ill for morals when fuch a character is thus indirectly held up to imitation by an author profeffing morality.

BENEATH this fplendid veil of engaging qualities, a vicious character lofes all its deformity

formity in the easily dazzled eyes of youth. In
Sophia's character, her sex find their sanction
for attaching themselves to a libertine; that
rock, on which female happiness is so often
wrecked.

HAVING thus enforced the obvious bad
tendency of the work, over which Mr. Cumberland pours so much applause, let us turn
to the volumes he *interdicts*, to the Clariffa of
Richardfon. It is no where that Morality is
more powerfully enforced; it is no where
that Piety is more exquifitely lovely. Every
individual in that large Dramatis Perfonæ, is
drawn with fuch diftinctnefs, fuch characteriftic ftrength, that not a letter, a fingle fpeech
in the whole work, but fo peculiarly belongs to
the nature of that fpirit, which is fuppofed to
have dictated it; that it is needlefs to caft the
eye back to the name of the fpeaker, or to
look at the fignature.

AMONGST the ftately family at Harlow-
Place, we do indeed perceive more precife,
and folemn ceremony than we find in the
houfes of country gentlemen at *this* period,
when Gallic eafe has ftolen upon the felf-im-
portance of the Britifh *'Squirality*; but every
body knows that fuch *were* the manners of
opulent country families, fome forty years

L   back,

back, where the mafter chofe to be the gentleman, rather than the toping and riotous
Foxhunter. Let it alfo be remembered, that
the Harlowes were a *new-raifed* family, that
wanted to eftablifh their *queftionably* dignity.

As to the perfifting authority, unjuftly
exercifed upon young women in the article of
marriage, *that* feature of probability in this
charming work, is ftill afcertained by a variety of examples every year, at leaft, in
wealthy, and ftill oftener in *high* life; though,
becaufe ceremony is not the *fafhion*, there
may be lefs *parade* in the *manner* of enforcing
it.

   " For rich-ones, with un'father'd eyes,
   " As Pride, or thirft of gold affail,
   " Attend their human Sacrifice,
   " Without the Grecian Painter's veil.

The author meant to hold up the portraits
of Clariffa, and Grandifon, to each fex, as
models of male, and female virtue. It has
been truly faid, that whatever be our aim,
whether the attainment of an art, of fcience,
or of virtue, the model, from which we copy,
cannot be too *perfect*. We might as well
blame the tranfcendant fculptor, as the mora-
lift; as rationally prefer lefs exquifite, lefs

beautiful

beautiful ſtatues, to the Venus de Medicis, and the Apollo Belvidere, becauſe they may be nearer reſemblances of the human form; as chuſe to contemplate a Jones, and a Sophia, rather than a Grandiſon, and a Clariſſa.

IF worn and hacknied in the tainted mazes of Society, *our* ardor for Virtue is grown palled, and ſick, ſo that we behold repreſentations of conſummate excellence without delight, let us not ſeek to deprive the generous credulity, and hoping ſenſibility of youth, of the nobleſt patterns our language affords (without the ſcriptural pale) of moral virtue, and piety; adorned and graceful in the charms of youth and beauty; in the ſplendor of elevated intellect; in the utmoſt elegance of ſtyle, and in all the intereſt of trying ſituations.

AN accurate obſerver of life and manners, muſt have many times beheld very exact reſemblances of every character in Clariſſa; the glorious maid, and her profligate raviſher alone excepted.

To form a bright example of female virtue, ſuperior to temptation in the great eſſential *chaſtity*; and in whom every leſſer conſideration of worldly fame and proſperity ſhould be ſubordinate to the delicacy of ex-

alted

alted principle; it was neceſſary to draw the character of *Lovelace*, exactly as he *is* drawn. Leſs accompliſhed, leſs brave, leſs bountiful, leſs eſtimable in all reſpects, (where his darling vice did not interfere) he could not have obtained the degree of intereſt he poſſeſſed in the heart of a Clariſſa; and without which, her reſiſtance had loſt all its merit. Leſs hardened by the power of this abſorbing vice, leſs determined, leſs cruelly perſiſting, ſhe could not have ſuſtained from him thoſe wrongs from which ſhe riſes ſo far above the Lucretian-chaſtity; evincing by her conduct the ſuperior excellence of the Chriſtian principles to thoſe which hurried into ſuicide the injured Roman matron.

As the *worſt* poſſible moral reſults from the character of Tom Jones, ſo does the *beſt* reſult from that of Lovelace. By the former, our youth are taught to believe that they may be very noble fellows, whom every body will love, and yet indulge their criminal appetites in the ſeduction of what they *believe* to be ruſtic innocence, as in Jones's amour with Molly Seagrim; and plunge into *known* adultery, as in his connection with Mrs. Waters; and this, even though they are in love with an amiable woman, as Jones with

Sophia.

Sophia.   A fituation, which infinitely en-
hances, and indeed renders wholly unpardon-
able the grofs, and brutal guilt of profligacy.
While by the character of Lovelace, as by
that of Macbeth, we are taught, that gallant
courage, and brilliant talents, form no fecu-
rity againft a man's becoming darkly villainous, if he deliver himfelf up, without re-
ftraint, to the influence of his conftitutional
vice.

WHILE the eye of fenfibility ftreams over
the fuffering, and over the dying Clariffa,
there is a " fecret, ftern, vindictive, yet not
" unjuft pleafure, that brightens thofe
" tears," and which always arifes in the generous bofom upon the punifhment of treachery, like that of Lovelace, and of inflexi-
bility like that of the Harlow-family.

COLD to the fenfe of devotion, dead to the
hope, and truft of a bleffed immortality, muft
be that heart, which does not triumph, and delight (however the eyes may overflow) in the
death of Clariffa, in the everlafting reft of a
broken heart, in the emancipation of an oppreffed, an injured, and angelic fpirit, foar-
ing above all its cruel perfecutors, to unfad-
ing light, and ever-during felicity.

L 3   N U M-

In Continuation.

MR. CUMBERLAND accuses this work of tedious prolixity, and the accusation is pretty general. It cannot be denied that even ingenious minds capable of perceiving its various excellencies, the graces of its eloquence, the powers of its pathos, and the brilliance of its wit, may, on a *first* perusal, find themselves so anxiously interested in the events, as to become impatient of any pause in the story.

BUT *recurring* to these volumes, (to which the sensible reader *will* recur as to Shakespear, to Milton, or the Rambler) when satisfied curiosity leaves the mind calm enough to remark, and enjoy at leisure their innumerable

rable

rable beauties; fomething will be found in *every* letter, which is highly curious and entertaining. In the mafter-ftrokes of truth, and nature, do they delineate the mind, and the manners of the fuppofed writer; befides throwing ftrong collateral light, and colouring, upon *other* characters in the work. This excellence of appropriation pervades all the epiftles, even thofe, in which elegance of ftyle is judicioufly abated, as in the letters of the proud, unyielding Harlowes; or wholly thrown afide, as in thofe of the proverbial Lord M——, the pedant Brand, and the menial perfonages; while, on this recurrent perufal, the characteriftic graces of the more *eloquent* epiftles fhine out, in Variety inexhauftible.

THE letters of *Lovelace* exhibit every gay attraction of peerlefs wit, picturefque defcription, claffic allufion, and univerfal knowledge, without any affectation in its difplay; a ftyle unrivalled in its eafy flow, and fafcinating harmony; and, what ftrikingly evinces the addrefs, and virtuous defign of the author, the epiftles of this feducing libertine, even more forcibly than any of the others, warn the youthful female againft the defigns of the oppofite Sex, by the ftartling axioms

L 4

they

they contain, refpecting the conduct of women. It is from the letters of *Lovelace*, that
they learn how inevitably defpicable they become in the eyes of thofe very men, to whofe
folicitations they are beginning to make facrifices, (apparently trivial) of that delicacy,
and purity fo lovely in the fex; facrifices
that generally end in the utter lofs of honour
from libertine encroachment.

In Colonel *Morden*'s letters, and in thofe
of Lovelace, and Belford, which defcribe the
colonel's perfon, his air, his manners, and his
conduct, we fee a perfect fine gentleman, in-
trepid and accomplifhed as the former, bene-
volent as the latter, and more virtuous;
while beneath the dignity which that virtue
confers, the dazzling *Lovelace* finks into vifible and confcious inferiority.

We find, in the touching epiftles of the
matchlefs Heroine of this work, the moft
complete powers of imagery and defcription,
fhaded over by that foft veil of diftrefs, thro'
which they appear with heightened grace,
and dearer intereft; the importance of every
duty that bleffes fociety; the danger and
mifery of every deviation from the path of
rectitude, enforced with the eloquence of an-
gels,—her character rifing amidft her fevere

trials,

trials, her deep diftreffes, and remorfelefs in-
juries, into unrivalled magnanimity;—while
in its nobleft elevation, the charm of female
foftnefs is never for a fingle moment loft.

MR. JEPHSON (perhaps our beft Tragedy-
writer fince Shakefpear) has availed himfelf,
in his poetic and fpirited tragedy Julia, of
the penknife-fcene in Clariffa. Deprived of
the preparatory circumftances that conftitute
a large part of its tranfcendant fublimity in
the *original* fituation, it could not but lofe ex-
tremely by the tranfpofition; but to thofe
who do not perfectly recollect the pages from
whence it is taken, the effect in the *Tragedy*
is very fine.

MR. CUMBERLAND tells the public, that
he knew a young female, whofe head was
turned by reading Clariffa; and who, in the
rage of imitation, infifted upon having her
coffin in her bed-chamber!

INSANE people have always fome reigning
idea. That the coffin of Clariffa fhould once
have proved that reigning idea, is furely a
very contemptible reafon for interdicting this
noble compofition, as inimical to the morals,
and difcretion of youth.

MANY religious enthufiafts have fancied
they had prophetic and apoftolic infpiration.
At the Cathedral of one of our celebrated
provincial towns, fome twenty years ago, I

often ufed to fee a man, whom many of the
prefent inhabitants remember. It was his
cuftom to ftand, during fervice, before the
rails of the altar. He had read about our
Saviour, till he fancied *himfelf* that facred
character, and a native refemblance of face,
and figure to the prints of Jefus, aided the
phrenzy. He had trained the growth of his
dark beard in the Jewifh fafhion, and his
hair, parted upon his forehead, hung in equal
ringlets down each fide the front part of his
neck. He was thin, and pale, with a remark-
able air of placid dignity. The mildnefs
this maniac conftantly preferved, rendered
him inoffenfive.

WITH the fame reafon might the SCRIP-
TURES be cenfured as a dangerous ftudy upon
that inftance, as this admirable work, becaufe
one romantic delirious fool befpoke her coffin,
without the reafons which impelled Clariffa
to take that fingular ftep.

IT is curious to hear the author of our
moft fentimental comedies, fpeak with contempt over the unerring fentiments which en-
rich thefe volumes. It would be happy for
the rifing, and for the future generation, if
our young women *would* imitate the principles, and the conduct of Clariffa, though

not

not perhaps in befpeaking their coffin: a cir-
cumftance for which fhe apologifes, con-
feffing it a fally of mournful enthufiafm,
and too fcrupulous delicacy; excufable *only*
from the peculiarity of her fituation, and
from being obliged to chufe a *male* executor.
Recommending Clariffa's conduct as an example, I defire it may be remembered that
her flight with Lovelace was involuntary,
and that her meeting and correfponding with
him, was merely from the perfecutions fhe
endured, and in the hope of preventing the
moft fatal mifchiefs between him and her brother.   She, however, repents of the two laft
circumftances, as forming a deep error, im-
ploring Heaven that its confequences may
warn her fex againft being rafh enough to
repofe the fmalleft degree of confidence in a
libertine; who, as fhe fays, to *be* a libertine
muft have got over and defied all moral
reftraints.

Is it from the pen of a *father* that we fee
the unfeeling, the pointlefs fneer upon the ex-
emplary duty, the contrite affection of a dying daughter, becaufe fhe writes *on her knees*
to fupplicate pardon for what fhe confiders a
great fault, that prohibited correfpondence
(though fhe had been impelled into the com-

milfion

miffion of it by the cruelty of her family) and to invoke bleffings upon them, who had fhewn no mercy to her!

In contradiction to experience, and with great illiberality, Mr. CUMBERLAND afferts, that encouraging young women to correfpond with each other, tends to no good point of education. *Every good habit is capable of being perverted to bad ufes.* Becaufe numerous books of evil tendency are extant, we might as wifely refolve that our daughters fhould not learn to *read*, as that, becaufe they *may* write frivolous, and improper letters, they fhould be precluded from the *certain* advantages of a well-regulated epiftolary intercourfe with their young friends. Difcreet parents will, in a great degree, fuggeft the fubjects of thefe letters, and invite from time to time, a communication of their contents, by expreffing pleafure in their perufal. Such an intercourfe forms the ftyle of young people, gives them habits of reflection, awakens intellectual emulation, and fupplies them with refources, which have an inevitable tendency to abate the defire of diffipation, enables them to be rational and pleafing companions to men of fenfe when they marry, to fill the parental and monitory duties with dignity

dignity and delight, to the certain improvement of the future generation.

IF women intrigue more in France than in England, though their understandings are generally better cultivated, it is because their inclinations are never consulted in their marriage engagements: and because infamy is less consequent than it is *here*, upon a violation of those engagements. But the French women are Lucretias compared to the Italians; a superiority which arises from the companionable qualities of the former, and the unlettered ignorance of the latter, that delivers up all the powers of their imagination to the influence of one reigning idea. Whoever has successfully studied the nature of the human mind, knows, that to store it with a *variety* of ideas, to render it capable of perceiving the value of knowledge, and the charms of genius, is to render it less subservient to the influence of the senses.

AFTER Mr. CUMBERLAND has expressed his desire of banishing the finest moral work of this age, from the libraries of our youth, and the pen from the fingers of our women; he proceeds to inveigh more justly against that mode of education, too prevailing within these last twenty years, which can never en-

large

large the ſtock of ideas, or inſpire any taſte for intellectual pleaſures. Upon this plan, a girl's time, in that important period, which divides infancy from womanhood, is every hour of it engroſſed by the French grammar, the harpſichord, the dancing, and the drawing-maſter.

WHEN young ladies *thus*, and *only* thus accompliſhed, become miſtreſſes, in any degree of their own time, whether ſingle, or married, there is no probability, alas! that they will devote it to the voluminous pages of the moral, the *pious* RICHARDSON. They have no imaginations that can awaken to a perception of his genius—no hearts that can ſoften at his pathos—no underſtanding to perceive the undeviating truth, and good ſenſe of his obſervations.

The Female Quixotte is an admirable ſatire upon the *now* totally exploded ſtudy of the old romances, and gave the death's wound to that declining taſte. But to ſatirize, with any probability of *good* effect, the CLARISSA, or the GRANDISON, is impoſſible. People of judgment will not attempt it, and injudicious people will attempt it in *vain*.

To read novels frequently, and indiſcriminately, is a moſt pernicious habit. There

are

are no means fo effectual of rendering them diftafteful as an early familiarity with the effufions of RICHARDSON's genius. They will exalt the underftanding above *endurance* of the trafh, daily pouring out from the circulating libraries. Who that has read MILTON waftes the midnight taper over the ——— ————Sir RICHARD BLACKMORE?

MR. CUMBERLAND does not want genius, though he will permit nobody to be *fenti-mental* but himfelf. His *very* fentimental comedies have confiderable merit, and though too little humorous for the comic line of writing, they are pathetic and agreeable. Morals are more likely to fuffer from our defpifing, than from our admiring them.

HIS tragedies have incurred more contempt than they deferve. Amidft frequent plagiarifms, and much turgid writing, there are fpeeches of unborrowed beauty, and ftriking imagery, both in the Battle of Haftings and in the Carmelite. Whole fcenes in the latter have the true dramatic fpirit.

JUDGMENT is this author's great defideratum. We perceive the want of that power in his own writings, and therefore need not wonder at its abfence, when he decides upon the writings of others.

UNDER

UNDER the influence of perpetually recurring infanity, the heroine of his Carmelite
preferves an important fecret through twenty
years, adheres to a regular plan of future en-
terprize, which is never interrupted by this in-
termitting madnefs, nor in the leaft degree
partakes of its influence. The author, who
could draw a character fo utterly out of nature, and probability, is likely enough to
fancy that RICHARDSON's works may be injurious to the good fenfe, the manners, and the
morals of our youth.

N U M B E R   XXVII.

WE cannot mention perhaps two motives of man's action, which, on a firſt view of them, appear ſo incompatible with each other, as thoſe of buſineſs and pleaſure : yet, where they are found uhiting in the ſame mind, their energies obtain one end. From ſuch an union (in the proportion that it is leſs expected) who is there that does not look the more for ſteadineſs in the purſuit, and ſupe-rior merit in the execution. As WALTER WEATHERCOCK, I feel all the ſpirit and reaſoning of the ſentence apply ; I am ſen-ſible, that, after having undertaken to offer *Variety* to the public, the doing it punc-tually, and in the ableſt manner, is not more a point of pleaſure, than it ſhould be of bu-ſineſs. In fact, both motives faſten an equal neceſſity on me ; and, like Cato, who al-

ways

ways concluded his old Punic ballad with the
" delenda eſt Carthago," the great burthen
to which my thoughts at laſt return is,
" *Variety muſt be furniſhed.*"

FULL of myſelf, and wrapt in the flatter-
ing conceit, that *Variety* had now *more than*
ever become neceſſary to the town, I was ſit-
ting a few evenings ago, *totus in illis*, in
full debate, on what ſhould be the ſubjeċt of
this our next Eſſay. I was yet unreſolved.
The entrance of a ſervant broke in upon my
doubts, and indeed, in the end, relieved
them. He delivered to me the ſeveral favours
of my correſpondents; I opened them as they
preſented themſelves, but when I took up
the packet which is the ſubjeċt of this paper,
I was a little ſtaggered on obſerving the im-
preſſion of the ſeal; a boar's head, in a field
verd, with the feet of a web-footed animal as
ſupporters, and the motto *nil mortalibus ar-*
duum eſt. My knowledge in heraldry did not
carry me ſo far, as to gueſs at the perſons of
my correſpondents; I therefore broke the
ſeal with ſome degree of curioſity; whether
my expeċtations were diſappointed or not, my
readers will determine, and as I had not
reſolved on my ſubjeċt, the following application was ſo novel a one, that I determined

to take the opinion of the world upon it, before I delivered my own in anfwer :

AND I fhall only requeft from my correfpondents, that the anfwer of the public be mine. In the multitude of counfellors there muft be wifdom, there muft be fafety; and Meffrs. the Petitioners are characters of too liberal a way of thinking, not to approve the trial by jury ; and in this confidence, we thus together put ourfelves upon the country.

THE HUMBLE PETITION of PEREGRINE SWINGTAIL and GREGORY WALKSTRAIT, more commonly called or known by the names of the *Learned Pig*, and the *Learned Goofe* ;

SHEWETH, ·

THAT encouraged by that liberal and amiable * fentiment, by which your firft Effay is diftinguifhed, your Petitioners have ventured to make their complaints and fears known, in the certainty that you will adminifter all the protection and comfort you can.

---

* The only difference between man and brutes, confifts in the folicitous demand for Variety.

THAT,

THAT, in this learned age, when the influence of knowledge and science is so universally felt, your Petitioners, among others, find themselves very much patronifed by the public; not fewer than one hundred of whom daily honour your Petitioners with their vifits, and not one of that hundred but departs fatisfied, with highly extolling your Petitioners improvement in *human reafon*.

THAT, owing to the meannefs of their fpecies, they are excluded from the common rights and enjoyments of *mankind*; and that your Petitioners' fenfibility often feel fhocked by the fear, that pride makes a component part of the applaufe which they receive, and that mankind fo applaud, becaufe they pity them. However, the confcioufnefs of worth is fuperior to a *little* conjecture againft another, and is therefore above fuppofing that another can apply fuch conjecture againft herfelf. Your Petitioners then are fatisfied on this fcore, and reft in the hope that the world will think as liberally as they do.

YOUR Petitioner GOOSE for himfelf faith, that he has reafon to efteem his knowledge, not only as the comfort, but as the *prefervation* of his life; for by an intenfe application to ftudy in his earlier days, he kept his *body*

in so continual a state of *leanness*, that it was
never judged *round or plump* enough for the
martyrdom of a spit, and hereby only has he
escaped the several anniversaries of that immortal foe to his race, *Saint Michael*; and,
when experience hath moulted every sickly
quill of folly from his wing, surely it would
now be hard to have his feathers rumpled
at an advanced age, by a rude premature
death; to prevent this evil, is now the great
mark of your petitioners wishes; and nothing
could effect it more firmly, than the throwing
open all the different professions to your Petitioners, by which they might reach the highest emoluments and offices in the state; nor
is there any justice in precluding them, since
they confess to have no scruples of conscience, but are willing to take all the *respec-
tive oaths* which the Test Act requires.

Your Petitioner *Goose*, therefore, further
says, that he can suggest no objection to his
being admitted to the study of the *Law*, and
in time becoming Attorney or Sollicitor-Gen-
eral; seeing too, that there are learned geese,
of every flock or drove, who have feathered
their nests by *hatches* not an egg more rational
than your Petitioner's might be. Your Petitioner cannot figure to his mind a reason why

he

he should not be Secretary at War or Commander in Chief, as well as any other goose among them; indeed your Petitioner is persuaded the army would be his *forte,* since without venturing much, he dares affirm that there is not a soldier or officer in his majesty's realm, who can *march* with so much *uprightness* as your Petitioner; and finally, since a man's family is often the best security for advancement in the army, your Petitioner flatters himself, he has some claim as a descendant of those Right Honourable Geese who stood centinals at, and saved the Capitol.

YOUR Petitioner *Pig,* for himself saith, that from the bitterness of his enemies the butchers (who would make brawn of any thing in the shape of flesh) he confesses that it has been with difficulty, he hath hitherto saved his bacon; and being desirous of still preserving the same, he feels a wish, in common with human nature, that his *grey hairs* (every *bristle* of which has been hoared in the service of science) may at last repose in an honoured grave.

AND your Petitioner begs to assure your HONOUR, that, notwithstanding the *swinish* superstition of the *herd* of Jews, your Petitioner has not a *slice of the Devil* in him. It

is

is then with diffidence he puts in a claim
thus to the public honours ; and touching the
feveral profeffions, your Honour knows that
the practice of *Medicine,* or art of killing, lies
in the licence to do it, viz. a diploma.   As
for the ftudy of *Botany,* all the town muft
acknowledge that no man can have a more
intimate acquaintance with the *vegetable world*
than your Petitioner, for this plain reafon,
becaufe he has the whole fyftem conftantly
under his nofe.   And further, his advantage
over thofe phyficians, who profefs to judge of
difeafes by infpecting the fecretions, cannot
be difputed, fince many allow that *pigs* can
fee the wind, and every one knows that they
have no falfe delicacy about tafting, or even
rolling themfelves in any filth whatever.

BUT, without enumerating all his merits,
which would look too much like vanity, your
Petitioner begs to clofe his claim with avow-
ing, that he thinks himfelf particularly qua-
lified to prefide at the Board of Ordinance,
from a conviction that he knows fomething
of fortification ; he having been all his life
fhut up by, and in contemplation of *walls* ;
and your Petitioner is fatisfied he could plan
as good a Stye to pen the nation up in, as
                                                  any

any of the works of Portsmouth or Ply-
mouth.

YOUR PETITIONERS, therefore, in all humility of posture, viz. Pig on his hocks,
and Goose on his giblets, most humbly
intreat your Honour to take the grievance
of their case into consideration, and to
advise or point out to them such relief,
as to your Honour shall seem *meat*; and
your Petitioners shall ever pray., &c.

IT is not necessary to our present purpose
to determine, whether vanity be a leading
step to vice, or a principal support of virtue.
There are opinions on each side of the question.   But where a man is the bigot to a favourite passion, and that passion a failing;
he seldom employs much industry to convince
either himself or the world that it is so; because, as soon as such conviction begins, his
failing ends; unless indeed he is so weak as
to be conscious that he is going to commit
an improper action, and yet wants resolution
to refrain from it.   From remarking the
little trouble I have taken, and seem inclined
to take on this score, every reader by this
time

time, perhaps, begins to anticipate a secret, which it is not my intention to keep from him; on the contrary, I shall freely confess (and without perceiving the smallest thrill of shame passing through me) that in my public capacity, I am as susceptible of vanity as the weakest of her devotees can be. Never did the mad heart of the extravagant Alexander feel a more acute pang of joy and triumph at the taking of a town, sacking of a city, or plundering of an empire, than Walter Weathercock would feel at the information, that he had made a single apostate from vice, or confirmed one wavering in the path of virtue.

WITH these sentiments about me, it is not difficult to imagine how much pleasure I received from the reflection that my very first essay should have been so serviceable; and such surely we must allow it to have been, when, through such means, two respectable members of society have found an opportunity of recording their claims on the world's approbation, and their *country's reward*. It will at least write this lesson in my memory, that benevolence of sentiment is often serviceable without a particular intention to be so, the opportunity of applying it when presented to us should never be passed over.

M Such

Such a character stands in the world like a beacon to guide wandering merit to her asylum, or shelter the friendless stranger from the storm, which Art and Interest are ever ready to pour on him.

N U M-

N U M B E R   XXVIII.

Mr. WEATHERCOCK.

YOU muſt know, Sir, that I am lineally deſcended from *Moſter Bottom*, the weaver, of whom ſuch honourable mention is made by the immortal Shakeſpeare, in his Midſummer Night's Dream: now, having a turn for poetry (by the way I am afraid this circumſtance may make ſome people ſuſpect, that the effect of the aſſe's head which Puck confered on my anceſtors, is not quite worn out) be this as it may, however, having, I ſay, a poetical turn, (or which is much the ſame thing) believing that I have, my genius *naturally* leads me to the Epigram, the merit of which ſpecies of compoſition is ſaid always

to·

to lie at the *bottom*, or, in other words, in the *tail*.

But, alas, Sir, however great the merit of the *Epigramatift* may be, he labours under one material difadvantage, if he wifhes to favour the world (as it is called) with his productions; for they are in general fo concife, that it would employ a man's whole life to produce Epigrams enough to fill a fhilling pamphlet, even though affifted (as moft modern books are) with a large type and ample margin. This has been hitherto a terrible obftacle to my ambition, but I am encouraged to hope, from the title of your paper, that I may arrive, through the medium of it, at the fummit of my wifhes, *viz.* the pleafure of difplaying my brilliant abilities to an admiring public.

Before I give you any fpecimen of my art, it may, perhaps, be advifeable to fay what an Epigram is, or rather what it ought to be; and this may probably be more eafily effected by mentioning what it is like, than by attempting to give a definition of it by words.

The Epigram, then, has been very aptly liken'd to a *fcorpion*, and to a *jelly bag*; your *Scorpion* Epigram includes all that may properly be ftiled fatyrical; that is to fay, thofe

that

that have a sharp sting in their tails : the *jelly
bag* will comprehend all the rest, namely, those
that are pointed at the end, but without any
acrimony whatever. Should a composition
claim the title of Epigram, without bearing
either of these essential marks, you may depend upon it, its title is without foundation ;
especially, if upon examination, it be found
to resemble a *sugar-loaf*, which is *pointed* at
the *wrong end*, or a *drum*, which is equally
flat at *both ends*; I am aware that most of the
poems handed down to us from the ancients,
under the name of Epigram, will appear (according to the modern acceptation of the
word) to rank in this latter class, and follow
the *drum :* but it should be remembered, that
the word, as now used, conveys a very different meaning from Επιγραμμα, which sig-
nified simply INSCRIPTION, and was equally applicable to prose and poetry ; every man
of taste must acknowledge the elegance of
many of these productions of antiquity ;
and it would be alike absurd to deny their
merit, because they do not answer to the
modern idea of Epigram, as to find fault
with the pathetic stories of *Lefevre*, or *la
Roche*, because there is nothing in either of
them that can excite laughter.

M 3

Your

Your correspondent, Philopun, compares the Pun and Epigram together, yet
seems not fully aware of their very near affi-
nity; but if the essence of the latter consists
in its *point*, then a *pun* is not only allowable,
but constitutes the chief merit of an Epigram; for, in the French language, the
words are synonimous. I am happy to find
my ideas confirmed by the great *Boileau Des-
peaux*. I will transcribe six lines from this,
admirable critic, because, while they justly
reprobate the use of a pun in serious discourse, they justify the introduction of one
occasionally in a lively Epigram.

Speaking of the shameful inundation of
puns or points which prevailed a few years
ago in every species of literature, he says,

" La raison outragée enfin ouvrit ses yeux
" La chassa pour jamais des discours serieux
" Et dans tous ces ecrits, la declarant infame,
" Par grace, lui laissa l'entrée en l'*Epigramme*."

Supported by such authority, I venture to
send you three of the jelly bag kind, and suppose, since your object is Variety, they
may find admission; but should any reader
have so squeamish a stomach, as to turn sick
at a pun, I advise him to pass them over, and
proceed

proceed to the fourth, which is of the fcorpion kind, and which I have inferted for the
fake of *Variety*: as I have no venom in me,
fo I do not take the merit of having written
the latter, but merely that of having extracted it from a newfpaper, as a curious inftance
.how feverely the moft amiable and beneficent
inftitution may become the objeƈt of keen
fatire.   I am,

Dear, Sir,

Your admirer

and humble fervant,

YOUNG BOTTOM.

J E L L Y B A G. No. I.

T H E verieft nothings kindle ftrife
'Twixt Plum, the grocer, and his wife;
Such quarrels, fure, are out of feafon,
For what's a *jar* without a *reafon*.

J E L L Y B A G. No. II.

AT a late exhibition, a taylor one day
His knowledge in painting began to difplay,
But one who ftood by that had fmelt out his trade,
Moft heartily laugh'd at the ftriƈtures he made;
Says a Wag, " Prithee, why fo contemptuoufly
      treat him ?
" I know in *Fine-drawing* there's none that can
      beat him."

JELLY

JELLY BAG, No. III.

OLD *John* was wedded to a crooked wife,
And thence was apprehenfive for his life,
Becaufe his brother *George* was forc'd to fly,
Charg'd with the heinous crime of *bigamy*;
" Alas !" quoth John, " I may have equal trouble,
" For tho' I've but one wife, God knows fhe's
    double."

No. IV.

THE SCORPION EPIGRAM,

*Addreffed to Sir John Millar, of Batheafton, on his
elegant plan of dedicating an Etrufcan Vafe for
the reception and encouragemet of poetic Effays.*

Miller! the URN in ancient times, 'tis faid
Held the collected *afhes* of the *dead*;
So thine (the wonder of thefe modern days)
* Stands open day and night for lifelefs lays:
Leave not unfinifh'd then the well form'd plan,
Complete the work thy claffic tafte began;
And oh ! in future, e're thou doft *inurn 'em*,
Remember firft, to *raife a pile* and *burn 'em.*

I SHALL

* Noctes atque dies patet atri janua ditis.

I SHALL add to my friend Young Bottom's communication, as applicable to the fubject, an Epigram of the late Dr. Johnfon, in Latin, with feven different tranflations by as many different perfons, which if they fhould all appear to belong to the *drum kind,* uniformly *flat* at both ends, they will at leaft furnifh the contemplative mind with an inftance of that *Variety* of words which may be ufed to convey the fame thought. The Epigram was written on the Temple of the Winds, built by Lord Anfon, at his feat at Shuckborough in Staffordfhire.

Gratum animum laudo, qui debuit omnia ventis
Quam bene ventorum, Templum Surgere jubet.

No. I.

Since to the winds alone, he ow'd the wealthy
    prize,
I praife the grateful foul that bade this temple rife.

No. II.

The grateful Anfon here adores the gales
That bore to wealth and power his fwelling fails.

M 5

No. III.

No. III.

From profp'rous winds, fince profp'rous fortune
    rofe,
This fane is rais'd to every wind that blows.

No. IV.

This Temple to the wind, his gratitude has rais'd,
As the wind gave him *all*, 'tis fit the wind be
    prais'd.

No. V.

Well, to the Winds, may he this fane afford,
Whom their propitious breath has made a lord.

No. VI.

No. VI.

Hail, thou great foul, whom gratitude bids raife,
This offering to the winds, which fwell'd thy
     praife.

No. VII.

The winds gave Anfon all, his very food,
And to the winds this marks his gratitude;
'Tis an ill wind indeed that blows no good.

N U M B E R   XXIX.

From a private Mad-house, Monday neareſt
the full Moon.

S I R,

HAVING lived long enough on this
earth to ſee the emptineſs of all enjoyments, the vanity of purſuits, and the un-
certainty of ſucceſs; I determined to riſk
every thing, and leave the world in ſearch
of a better: but, though I was diſguſted
with the *world*, I had not quarrelled with
life; I did not follow the example of my
countrymen in hanging or drowning myſelf;
no, Sir, I reſolved to take advantage of the
late wonderful diſcoveries in chymiſtry, and

turn

turn my back on one globe, by the help of another; so I provided myself with a magnificent balloon.

My principal object was to visit one of the planets, and I thought I might reach the *Moon* in a very short time; but, as a prudent man always guards against the possibility of failure in the best planned undertaking, so I had prepared myself with every necessary to execute another scheme, should my original one prove abortive, and this was the taking a trip to the *East Indies*; which, by the help of these machines, is easily to be done in about eight hours. Here, lest the stupidity of future Æronauts may not see the facility of this voyage, I will explain it in a manner to be comprehended by the meanest proficient in Natural Philosophy.—Nothing more is necessary, than to ascend in a perpendicular direction, till the balloon is out of the earth's attraction; then remain stationary about eight hours, and descend in the same direction; the earth will in that time have revolved one-third upon its axis, and this will land you somewhere in the East Indies.—From thence to England the return is to be made in the same manner, allowing sixteen hours instead of eight for the remaining

ing two-thirds of the earth's circumference;
for as every body knows that the earth re-
volves on its own axis once in twenty-four
hours, it is felf-evident that the effect muft
be the fame, whether a man go round the
world till he come to the fame fpot, or whether he ftands ftill, and lets the world go
round without him, till the fame fpot returns
to him.   But to proceed with the account of
my voyage.

HAVING filled my balloon, and taken my
feat in the car, I cut the lines which faftened
it to the ground, and away I flew like a cork
from a bottle of Champaigne.—I will not
detain you with defcriptions of the country
I had quitted, the clouds under me like
fleeces of wool, or the intenfe heat and cold
of the mediums through which I paffed for
the firft few miles, they being already fo
amply related by others; I fhall only obferve,
that my remarks confirmed theirs as far as
they went, particularly with refpect to the
power of afcenfion being augmented as the
air became more rarified; for the velocity of
my progrefs increafed fo rapidly, that at
length, by my calculation, I found I was
going fafter than a ball fired from the largeft
cannon, in the proportion of $736\frac{7}{17}$ to 1,

and

and this convinced me I fhould reach the moon before fun-fet.

I EXPECTED, as I approached this novel regicn, to be charmed with that *variety* of colours and objeƈts which the earth prefents to the delighted Æronaut; but, on the contrary, the whole furface feemed one uniform mafs of the brighteft filver, and thofe apparent fpots and ftreaks which have induced the learned to fancy they faw hills and valleys, and which the ignorant believe to be a man with a faggot on his back, were now proved to be the illufions of imagination, or the deception of fight.—I particularly noticed the three luminous fpots which the ingenious HERSCHELL has fuppofed to be volcanoes; but, as I approached them, they appeared no longer *three*, but *one*—and they became a ftriking proof how abfurdly men are apt to argue from analogy, and how vain are all conjeƈtures refpeƈting heavenly and incomprehenfible fubjeƈts, when founded on apparent fimilitude to what we fee on earth. I fhall therefore here premife, that when I ufe familiar comparifons or allufions to explain what I have feen, you muft not underftand me literally; for, in defcribing things which were never heard or feen, or even thought of

before,

before, there muſt inevitably be great difficulty to convey adequate ideas.

I LANDED on the plated ſurface of the moon, at ſeven o'clock P. M. and walked about three miles before I ſaw the ſmalleſt hope of finding it inhabited; at length I diſcovered an *intellectual* SOMETHING, for I cannot call it *Matter*, becauſe it had no parts; nor *Spirit*, becauſe it ſeemed materially viſible: in ſhort, if I muſt compare it to any thing we know, it muſt be to an intelligent and ſparkling HUMAN EYE. That you may underſtand me, Sir, I muſt aſk, if you have never ſeen a *human eye* which could convey the ſeveral ideas of love, or fear, or pride, or anger, with a ſingle look? and, without the help of language, could expreſs the ſtrongeſt pleaſure or diſguſt? Such, in a degree beyond human conception, was the object I am deſcribing, and with which I held a converſe purely intellectual; for it anſwered my enquiries, and ſatisfied my utmoſt curioſity, before I had time to form my queſtions into words. Of this almoſt intuitive conference the reſult was this:—that in the moon there is no *variety*; a perfect *ſameneſs* dwells throughout the extenſive regions of this mighty luminary, conſequently it can

only

only be inhabited by a fingle perfon; for it is impoffible for two things, however nearly refembling each other, to exift without diftinction.

THE three fuppofed volcanoes, therefore, are but one great glare, the fole ufe of which is to keep up an uniformity of light and warmth during the abfence of the fun; for here is no difference betwixt day and night, or betwixt heat and cold.   Upon farther enquiry into the ftate of exiftence in a country where *perfect uniformity* prevailed, I found there was neither *pain*, nor *fear*, nor *forrow:* but while I was going to rejoice in being admitted into fuch a ftate of happinefs, I was told by a look, that there was alfo neither *pleafure*, *hope*, nor *joy*; for that each could only exift by comparifon with its contrary: and that all the *variety* which proceeds from health and ficknefs, power and dependance, company and folitude, with all that inexhauftible fund of contrarieties which form the various fhades betwixt GOOD and EVIL on our globe, derived their very being from the power of *contraft*; and that where *perfect uniformity* prevailed, neither happinefs nor mifery could be long expected.

FOR

FOR some time, the satisfaction I received in this intellectual converse seemed to contradict the last assertion, for the novelty of such instruction gave me happiness which I could not suppress. To find myself at once at the fountain-head of science; to learn without application, and to know without research; to investigate without fatigue, and to discover without the trouble of seeking, appeared to me such never-failing sources of true delight, that I was about to express the transports I experienced, and dispute the point with my antagonist, when the eye glanced contempt.—I felt at once the narrowness of my discernment, blushed to be confuted by a look, and shrunk into myself with shame at my defeat; then cheered again, and (like the disturbed quickfilver of a barometer) my spirits for a time fluctuated betwixt *joy* and *mortification*, till at last they settled in perfect *indifference.* This put an end to our conference, and left me in that listless indolence of mind which can only be roused by the calls of nature.

I WAS going to ask, if supper was not ready? when another look of contempt informed me, that hunger was a source of *variety* unknown to my new acquaintance; and

I shut

I ſhut my eyes, that I might be no longer expoſed to this intuitive converſation. 'T was then I devoutly wiſhed for the means of returning to my own planet, where life is chequered by the never-ceaſing pleaſures of *novelty* and *change*; where *corporeal refreſhments* add vigour to the *ſoul*, and *mental extacy* is joined with *ſenſual appetite*; where unexpected *joy* ſucceeds the pangs of *ſorrow*, and where through *pain* we reach our higheſt *pleaſure*; where hateful *vice* ſets off the charms of *virtue*; and where preſent *calamities* and *evil* give way to future proſpects of never-ending *happineſs*.

Thus meditating in the preſence of that eye which I dared no longer conſult, I inſenſibly fell aſleep, and, by ſome unknown power, was ſuddenly tranſported (together with the ſhattered fragments of my balloon) to my own garden from whence I took my flight.

Oh! Sir, you will ſcarce believe me, when I tell you how ungratefully my nephew uſes me; I have brought him up, and educated him to be my heir; and this boy, inſtead of being pleaſed at my return, and liſtening with rapture to my wonderous narrative, proclaims to all the world that I am

mad,

mad, and has artfully converted my adventures to his advantage, by making it a plea for putting me into this house, that he may put himself into possession of my estate.

IF you are not displeased with my correspondence, you may expect to hear from me again; in the mean while, do me the justice to believe that I am,

S I R,

Your's in truth,

L U N A T I C U S.

N U M-

N U M B E R XXX.

THE FRIAR's TALE.

IN feveral convents fituated among the mountains which divide France and Italy, a cuftom prevails that does honour to human nature: in thefe fequeftered cloifters, which are often placed in the moft uninhabited parts of the Alps, ftrangers and travellers are not only hofpitably entertained, but a breed of dogs are trained to go in fearch of wanderers, and are every morning fent from the convents with an apparatus faftened to their collars, containing fome refrefhment, and a direction to travellers to follow the fagacious animal: many lives are by this means preferved in this wild romantic country. During my laft vi-

fit

fit to the South of France, I made a trip into this mountainous region, and at the convent of * * *, where I was at firft induced to prolong my ftay by the majeftic fcenery of its Environs; as that became familiar, I was ftill more forcibly detained by the amiable manners of the reverend Father, who was at that time Superior of that monaftery: from him I received the following pathetic narrative, which I fhall deliver, as nearly as I can recollect, in his own words.

'About twenty years ago, (faid the ve-
'nerable old man) I was then in the 57th
'year of my age, and fecond of my priority
'over this houfe, a moft fingular event
'happened through the fagacity of one of
'thefe dogs, to which I became myfelf a wit-
'nefs. Not more than a dozen leagues from
'hence, there lived a wealthy gentleman, the
'father of *Matilda*, who was his only child,
'and whofe hiftory I am going to relate.
'In the fame village lived alfo *Albert*, a youth
'poffeffed of all the world deems excellent
"in man, except one fingle article, which
'was the only object of regard in the eyes
'of *Matilda*'s father. *Albert*, with a graceful
'perfon, cultivated mind, elegance of man-
'ners, and captivating fweetnefs of difpo-
'fition,

' fition, was poor in fortune; and *Matilda's*
' father was blind to every other considera-
' tion; blind to his daughter's real happi-
' nefs, and a ftranger to the foul-delighting
' fenfation, of raifing worth and genius, de-
' preffed by poverty, to affluence and inde-
' pendence. Therefore on *Matilda's* confef-
' fion of unalterable attachment to her be-
' loved *Albert,* the cruel father refolved to
' take advantage of the power which the laws
' here give a man, to difpofe both of his
' *daughter* and his *wealth* at pleafure; the lat-
' ter he refolved to bequeath to his nephew
' *Conrad,* and *Matilda* was fent to a neigh-
' bouring convent; where, after a year's pro-
' 'bation, fhe was to be compelled to renounce
' 'both *Albert* and the world.

   ' CONRAD, whofe artful infinuations had
' long worked on the weak mind of this mif-
' guided father, was not content with hav-
' ing thus feparated thefe lovers, but by in-
' 'citing perfecution from the petty creditors
' of *Albert,* drove him from his home; and,
' after many fruitlefs endeavours to commu-
' nicate with his loft miftrefs, he fled for
' fanctuary to this convent. Here (faid the
' hoary monk) I became acquainted with the

' virtues

' virtues of that excellent young man, for he
' was our gueſt about ten months.

- ' In all this time *Matilda* paſſed her days
' in wretchedneſs and perſecution ; the abbeſs
' of her convent, Siſter *Thereſa*, who, to the
' diſgrace of her profeſſion and our holy
' church, diſguiſed the diſpoſition of a devil
' in the garment of a ſaint ; became the friend
' and miniſter of *Conrad*'s wicked purpoſes,
' and never ceaſed to perſecute *Matilda*
' by falſe reports concerning *Albert*, urging
' her to turn her thoughts from him, to
' that heavenly ſpouſe to whom ſhe was about
' to make an everlaſting vow. *Matilda* ſcorn-
' ed her artifice, and love for *Albert* reſiſted
' every effort of the abbeſs to ſhake her con-
' fidence in his fidelity.

' She was in the laſt week of her novici-
' ate, when her father became dangerouſly
' ill, and deſired once more to ſee her. *Con-*
' *rad* uſed every endeavour to prevent it,
' but in vain ; ſhe was ſent for ; and the inter-
' view was only in the preſence of *Conrad*
' and the nurſe ; but when the dying father
' perceived the altered countenance of his
' once beloved child, his heart condemned
' him, he reflected that the wealth which he
' was going to quit for ever, belonged to her,

' and

‘ and not to *Conrad*, and he resolved to ex-
‘ piate his cruelty by cancelling the will,
‘ and consenting to the union of *Albert* and
‘ *Matilda*.   Having made a solemn decla-
‘ ration of his purpose, he called for the
‘ will ; then taking *Matilda*’s hand in one of
‘ his, and presenting the fatal writing with
‘ the other, he said, “ Forgive thy father !
“ destroy this paper, and be happy ; so be my
“ sins forgiven in heaven !”   ‘ The joy of
‘ his heart at this first effort of benevolence,
‘ was too much for his exhausted spirits, and
‘ he expired as he uttered the last words,
‘ letting fall the will, which he was going to
‘ deliver.

‘ MATILDA’s gentle soul was torn with
‘ contending passions, she had lost her father
‘ at the moment when he had bestowed fresh
‘ life ; and, in the conflict betwixt joy and
‘ grief, she sunk on the lifeless corps, in an
‘ agony of gratitude and filial tenderness.

‘ MEANWHILE *Conrad* did not let slip this
‘ opportunity to compleat his plan, which, by
‘ the dying words of his uncle had been so
‘ nearly defeated ; he secured the will, and
‘ corrupted the nurse by promises and bribes,
‘ never to reveal what she had witnessed ;
‘ half persuading the interested doating old

N   ‘ woman,

‘ woman, that it was only the effect of deli-
‘ rium in the deceafed. This idea was but
‘ too well fupported by the firft queftion of
‘ *Matilda*, who exclaimed, as fhe came to
‘ herfelf ; “ Where am I ! fure ’tis a dream !
“ my father could not fay I fhould be happy,
“ he could not bid me tear that fatal will ?
“ Speak ! am I really awake, or does my fan-
“ cy mock me with fuch founds ?” The
‘ artful *Conrad* affured her that nothing of
‘ the kind had paffed, telling her that her fa-
‘ ther had only mentioned *Albert*’s name to
‘ curfe him ; and, with his laft breath, com-
‘ manded her to take the veil at the expira-
‘ tion of the week. All this the perjured
‘ nurfe confirmed ; and then *Matilda*, being
‘ perfectly recovered, firft faw the horrors
‘ of her fituation. It was in vain for her to
‘ deny what they afferted, or remonftrate
‘ againft their combined perfidy. She was
‘ prefently, by force, again conveyed to her
‘ nunnery, in a ftate of mind much eafier to
‘ imagine than defcribe.

‘ HERE fhe was more violently than ever
‘ attacked by *Therefa*’s perfecution, who urg-
‘ ed with increafing vehemence, the pretend-
‘ ed pofitive commands of her dying father ;
‘ and, by the advice of *Conrad*, ufed feveri-

‘ ties

' ties of conventual difcipline, which almoft
' robbed the devoted victim of her reafon;
' ftill pleading, that RELIGION juftified her
' conduct. Can it be wondered, that fuch
' cruel treatment fhould at length difturb the
' piety and faith of poor *Matilda?* and in-
' duce her to exclaim, with prefumptuous
' bitternefs, againft the holy inftitutions of our
' church, and brand the facred ordinances
' of our religion with unjuft fufpicions.
" Why! (faid fhe) why are thefe maffy
" grates permitted to exift, why are thefe
" hated walls fad prifons of innocence and
" youth, where fraud and cruelty have power
" to torture and confine the helplefs? RELI-
" GION is the plea; Religion! which fhould
" bring peace, and not affliction, to its vo-
" taries; then furely that religion which
" juftifies thefe gloomy dungeons muft be
" falfe, and I will abjure it; yes! I will fly
" to happier regions, where prifons are alot-
" ted only to the guilty; there, no falfe vows
" to heaven are exacted, but *Albert* and *Ma-*
" *tilda* may be yet happy." ' The poffibili-
' ty of an efcape had never before prefented
' itfelf, and indeed, it could never have oc-
' cured but to one whofe reafon was difor-
' dered, for fhe well knew that the doors
N 2   ' were

' were fecured by many bars and locks, and
' that the keys were always depofited beneath
' the pillow of the Abbefs.

   ' Her imagination was now too much heat-
' ed to attend to any obftacles, and with a
' mixture of forefight, infpired by infanity,
' fhe packed up all her little ornaments of
' value, carelefsly drew on her cloaths, and
' put in her pocket fome bread and provifion
' which had been left in her cell; then wrap-
' ping round her elegant form one of the
' blankets from the bed, fhe lighted a taper,
' and fearlefs walked towards the Cloifter door,
' idly expecting that it would fly open of its
' own accord, to innocence like hers—and
' now methinks I fee her, with hair difhevel-
' led, face pale and wan, her large black eyes
' wildly ftaring, and the whole of her ghaft-
' ly figure, lighted by the feeble glimmer of
' her taper, majeftically ftalking through the
' gloomy vaulted hall; arrived at the great
' door, fhe found it partly open, and fcarce
' believing what fhe faw, fhe quickly glided
' through it; but, as fhe paffed, an iron bar
' which fhe had not obferved, and which
' projected at the height of her forehead,
' flightly grazed her temple; and though fhe
' fcarcely felt the wound, yet it added new
                        ' horrors

‘ horrors to her look, by covering her ghoſt-
‘ like face with ſtreaks of blood.

  ‘ ALTHOUGH *Matilda* had never conſider-
‘ ed the improbability of paſſing this door,
‘ ſhe now reflected with wonder how ſhe had
‘ paſſed it, and fear of a diſcovery began to
‘ operate, as ſhe with more cautious ſteps
‘ moved ſilently through the cloiſter towards
‘ the outer-gate; which when ſhe approached,
‘ ſhe heard *Thereſa*’s voice whiſpering theſe
‘ words : “ Adieu, dear *Conrad* ; but remem-
“ ber that your life, as well as mine, depend
“ on the ſecrecy of our conduct:” ‘then
‘ tenderly embracing each other, a man
‘ ran ſwiftly from her, and the Abbeſs turn-
‘ ing round, ſtood motionleſs with horror
‘ at the bloody ſpectre firmly approach-
‘ ing. The guilty mind of *Thereſa* could only
‘ ſuppoſe the horrid viſion to be the departed
‘ ſpirit of one whom ſhe thought her cruelties
‘ had murdered ; and while the panic ſeized
‘ her whole frame, a guſt of wind from the
‘ gate, extinguiſhing the taper, *Matilda* ſeem-
‘ ed to vaniſh, as ſhe reſolutely puſhed thro’
‘ the poſtern door ſtill open.

  ‘ THERESA was too well hackneyed in the
‘ ways of vice, to let fear long take poſſeſ-
‘ ſion of her prudence : the night was dark,

N 3   and

' and it would have been in vain to purfue
' the phantom, if her recovering courage had
' fuggefted it; fhe therefore refolv'd to faften
' both the doors, and return in filence to her
' own apartment, waiting, in all the pertur-
' bation of anxiety and guilt, till morning
' fhould explain this dreadful myftery.

　' Meanwhile *Matilda*, confcious in her in-
' nocence, and rejoicing in her efcape, pur-
' fued a wandering courfe through the un-
' frequented paths of this mountainous dif-
' trict, during three whole days and nights;
' partly fupporting her fatigue by the provi-
' fions fhe had taken with her, but more from
' a degree of infanity, which gave her powers
' beyond her natural ftrength; yet, in her
' diftracted mind, this laft inftance of *The-*
' *refa*'s wickednefs, had excited a difguft and
' loathing, bordering on fury againft every
' *Religious* or *Monaftic inftitution*.'

THE Monk had proceeded thus far, when
he was called away to attend the duties of
his convent, and promifed to continue the
narrative at his return.

NUMBER XXXI.

THE FRIAR's TALE

(Continued.)

THE Father foon returned, and proceeded with his narrative as follows:

'DURING the whole twelve months of
' *Matilda*'s noviciate, no intercourfe of any
' kind had paffed betwixt her and *Albert*,
' who continued under the protection of this
' houfe, alike ignorant of her father's death,
' and of all the other tranfactions which I
' have now related: yet knowing that the

' term of her probation was about to expire,
' he refolved once more to attempt fome
' means of gaining admittance to her con-
' vent. With this view he made a journey
' thither in the difguife of a peafant; and,
' on the very morning in which his miftrefs
' had efcaped, he prefented himfelf at the
' gate.

' CONRAD, who had by letter from the
' Abbefs been informed that her prifoner was
' fled, was defired to come immediately, and
' devife fome excufe to the fifters for what
' had happened; for, although both to *Conrad*
' and *Therefa* the fact was evident enough,
' yet the fifter nuns were diftracted in con-
' jectures: till, by one of thofe artful ftretches
' of affurance, which confummate villainy
' finds it eafy to exert, *Conrad* recommended
' a plaufible expedient.—And now RELIGION
' (that conftant comfort of the good, and
' powerful weapon of the wicked) prefented
' itfelf, as the only refource in this emer-
' gency. *Therefa* was taught to fay (for the
' prefent), that fhe had no doubt the finful
' reluctance of *Matilda* to receive the veil
' had excited the wrath of Heaven; and that
' fhe was miraculoufly fnatched away, or
' perhaps annihilated, to prevent the dread-
' ful

‘ ful profanation of the holy ceremony at
‘ which she must that day have affisted.

‘ THIS plan had been settled, and *Conrad*
‘ was going with all haste in pursuit of the
‘ fugitive, when, at the outer gate, he met
‘ the pretended peasant.—The penetrating
‘ eye, either of Love or Hatred, soon discovers
‘ a friend or enemy, however carefully dis-
‘ guised—*Conrad* and *Albert* knew each other.
‘ —Instantly the flames of hatred, jealousy
‘ and fury, kindled in their bosoms; and
‘ *Conrad* seizing *Albert* by the throat, ex-
‘ claimed, “ I’ve caught the villain, the
“ sacrilegious ravisher!”—A severe struggle
‘ ensued, in which *Conrad* drew his sword;
‘ but *Albert* (who had no weapon) dextrously
‘ wrenched the instrument from the hand of
‘ *Conrad*, and plunged it in his bosom.—The
‘ villain fell; while *Albert* fled with the ut-
‘ most precipitation from the bloody scene,
‘ and returned in the evening to this con-
‘ vent.

‘ How shall I describe (said the good old
‘ Monk) the contrast betwixt the looks of
‘ our unhappy youth at this moment, and on
‘ the preceding morning when he left us!—
‘ Then, innocence faintly enlightened by a
‘ gleam of hope, smiled in his features, as

N 5

‘ he

‘ he chearfully bid us adieu, and said, “ per-
“ haps I may again hear tidings of *Matilda*,
“ fhould the will of Heaven deny me happi-
“ nefs with her, I will come back refigned,
“ and dedicate my future life to holy medi-
“ tation void of guilt.” But now, he re-
‘ turned breathlefs and pale, his hands be-
‘ fmeared with. blood, his limbs trembling;
‘ he could only utter, in faultering words,
“ Save me, reverend Fathers! fave me from
“ juftice, from myfelf, if poffible! Behold a
“ murderer!”

‘ SOME hours elapfed before we could col-
‘ lect from him, the circumftances of a crime,
‘ which had produced this extreme degree of
‘ horror and compunction in a mind fo vir-
‘ tuous and innocent as that of *Albert*; and,
‘ having heard the whole, in which he took
‘ all the blame to his own hafty conduct, we
‘ promifed him protection; and endeavoured,
‘ though in vain, for two whole days to
‘ fpeak comfort to his troubled mind, and to
‘ infpire confidence in the boundlefs mercy
‘ of his GOD. On the third day we were
‘ diverted from this arduous tafk, by the
‘ return and behaviour of one of our dogs;
‘ the poor animal, who had been out all day,
‘ was reftlefs, and fhewed evident marks of
‘ a defire that we fhould accompany him to
‘ the

‘ the relief of some poor wretch, who was
‘ unable to reach our convent.

    ‘ Father Jerome and I resolved to fol-
‘ low him; and we proceeded about half a
‘ mile when we turned from the beaten
‘ track guided by our dog, to a retired glen
‘ where human feet had hardly ever trod
‘ before.—Here, on a rock, which projected
‘ over a dreadful precipice, sat an unhappy
‘ half-distracted object; I need not tell you,
‘ it was *Matilda.*—She had crept with won-
‘ derous difficulty up a steep ascent to a ledge
‘ of rock which overhung a fearful chasm
‘ (the very recollection of the place freezes
‘ my blood!) when we first discovered her,
‘ she was eagerly clinging to a branch of
‘ yew which grew from a fissure in the rock
‘ above, and which half shaded her melan-
‘ choly figure.

    ‘ The dog followed her steps; but *Jerome*
‘ and I, unable to ascend a path so dangerous,
‘ stood unobserved by her, at a little distance
‘ on the opposite side the glen.

    ‘ When *Matilda* first perceived the dog,
‘ she looked with wildness round her; then
‘ fixing her eyes with tenderness on the
‘ animal, she said, “ Are you returned to me
“ again? and are you now my friend? Fie,

" fie upon it! Shall even dogs seduce the
" helpless!—Perhaps you repent of what
" you would have done—You look piteously.
" Alas! *Matilda* can forgive you!—Poor
" brute! you know I followed you all the
" day long, and would have followed you
" for ever, but that you led me to a de-
" tested convent!—Thither *Matilda* will not
" go—Why should *you* lead me to a prison?
" a dog cannot plead RELIGION in excuse
" for treachery!" She paused; then taking
' a rosary of pearls from her side, she fan-
' tastically wound it about the dog's neck,
' saying, " I have a boon to ask, and thus I
" bribe you; these precious beads are yours:
" now guide me to the top of this high
" mountain, that I may look about me, and
" see all the world.—Then I shall know
" whether my *Albert* still be living—Ah, no!
" it cannot be! for then *Matilda* would be
" happy! and that can never, never he!"
' She then burst into a flood of tears, which
' seemed to give her some relief.

' WHEN I thought she was sufficiently
' composed, *Jerome* and I discovered our-
' selves. On this she shrieked, and hid her
' face; but calling to her, I said, " *Albert* is
" still alive." She looked at us, till by
' degrees

‘ degrees ſhe had wildly examined us from
‘ head to foot; then turning to the dog, ſhe
‘ ſeized him by the throat, and would have
‘ daſhed him down the precipice, ſaying,
“ Ah, traitor! is it thus thou haſt betrayed
“ me?”—But the animal ſtruggled and got
‘ from her. She then firmly looked at us,
‘ and cried, “ Here I am ſafe, deceitful mon-
“ ſters! ſafe from the tyranny of your reli-
“ gious perſecution; for, if you approach
“ one ſingle ſtep, I plunge into this yawning
“ gulph, and ſo eſcape your power.—Ha!
“ ha! ha!”—Then recovering from a frantic
‘ laugh, ſhe ſaid, “ Yet tell me, did you not
“ ſay that *Albert* lives? Oh! that ſuch words
“ had come from any lips but thoſe of a falſe
“ monk!—I know your arts; with *you* ſuch
“ falſehoods are religious frauds; this is a
“ pious lie, to enſnare a poor helpleſs linnet
“ to its cage: but I tell you, cunning prieſts!
“ here I defy you; nor will I ever quit this
“ rock, till *Albert*’s voice aſſures me I may
“ do it ſafely.”

‘ You will eaſily imagine (continued the
‘ monk) the ſituation of *Jerome* and myſelf.
‘ Ignorant then of the manner in which
‘ *Matilda* had eſcaped, we could only know
‘ from her words and actions that it was ſhe
‘ herſelf,

‘ herfelf, and that her fenfes were impaired ;
‘ perplexed how to entice her from this pe-
‘ rilous retreat, and knowing that one falfe
‘ ftep would dafh her headlong down the
‘ dreadful chafm that parted us, at length
‘ I faid, “ Gentle maid, be comforted; *Albert*
“ and *Matilda* may yet be happy.” Then
‘ leaving *Jerome* concealed among the bufhes
‘ to watch the poor lunatic, I haftened to the
‘ convent, to relate what I had feen.

‘ MEANWHILE, *Matilda* looking with va-
‘ cant ftare around her, from time to time
‘ repeated my words, “ *Albert and Matilda*
“ *may yet be happy;*” then paufing, fhe feemed
‘ delighted with the found re-echoed from
‘ the rocks, again repeating, “ *Albert and*
“ *Matilda may yet be happy;*” ftill varying
‘ the modulation of her voice, as joy, grief,
‘ doubt, defpair, or hope alternately prevailed
‘ in her difordered mind.’

AT this interefting period of the narrative,
the venerable father was a fecond time called
out, and promifed to conclude his ftory when
he returned.

N U M B E R   XXXII.

T H E   F R I A R's   T A L E,

(Concluded.)

' I WILL not long detain you (refumed
' the Reverend Friar) with the effect my
' narrative had on the dejected *Alert*, how
' he at firft exclaimed, " Can there be com-
" fort for a guilty wretch like *Albert?*" and
' eagerly ran towards the place; then moved
' more calmly on my reprefenting how fatal
' might be furprize to one in fo dangerous a fi-
' tuation ; and at length fhrinking back, as he
' approached the fpot, and turning to me, he
' faid, " Father, I will go no further! Hea-
" ven has ordained, as a punifhment for the
                                    " murder

"murder I have committed, that I should
" become a witnefs to the fhocking death of
" the poor loft *Matilaa* ; at my approach, in
" frantic extafy fhe will quit her hold, and
" perifh before my fight." I urged him to
' proceed, but it was in vain, he fat down on
' a bank, and was filently wrapt in an agony
' of irrefolution, when he heard, at a little
' diftance, the well known voice of the poor
' lunatic, ftill repeating my words; " *Al-*
" *bert and Matilda may yet be happy.*" Roufed
' by the found, he ftarted up, and cautioufly
' advancing, he exclaimed ; " Juft Heaven !
" fulfil thofe words, and let them, indeed, be
" happy !"

' MATILDA knew the voice, and carefully
' treading a path, which would have feemed
' impracticable to one poffeffed of reafon, fhe
' defcended from the ledge on which fhe fat,
' and approached with cautious fteps ; but,
' at the fight of *Albert*, fhe flew impetuoufly
' forward, till feeing me, fhe as fuddenly
' ran back, and would have again retreated to
' the rock, fhrieking, " It is all illufion !
" prieftcraft ! it is no real *Albert*, and I am
" betrayed." We purfued, and caught her ;
' then finding my religious garb augmented
' the diforder of her mind, I withdrew, leav-
' ing only *Albert* to calm her needlefs fears.

' BUT

' BUT no perfuafion, even from him, could'
' induce her to come within view of the
' convent gates; I provided, therefore, ac-
' commodations for her in the cottage of a
' labourer, at fome little diftance; where, for
' many days, her delirium continued, while
' a fever threatened a fpeedy diffolution. Du-
' ring this period, *Albert* was labouring un-
' der all the anxiety which his fituation could
' infpire; the deed he had committed fat
' heavy on his foul, and he dared not hope
' for an event, which his own guilty thoughts
' reproached him with having not deferved.

' At length the crifis of the fever fhew'd
' figns of a recovery, and now his joys was
' without bounds, even the blood of *Conrad*
' feemed a venial crime, and he triumphed in
' the anticipation of reward for all he had
' fuffered: but this happinefs was of fhort
' duration, for at that time I received a let-
' ter from the Abbefs *Therefa*, demanding
' back the fugitive, whofe retreat fhe had dif-
' covered. This requifition I knew I muft
' obey; and giving the letter to *Albert*, I was
' going to explain the neceffity of my com-
' pliance, when he burft out in bitter exe-
' crations againft this and all *religious houfes*;
' curfing their eftablifhment as a violation of
' the

' the firſt law of nature, which commands
' an intercourſe betwixt the ſexes.

' HAVING heard, with a mixture of pa-
' tience, pity, and reſentment, all that his
' rage or diſappointment could ſuggeſt, I an-
' ſwered nearly in theſe words, beginning
' calmly, but by degrees aſſuming all the
' authority the caſe required : " My ſon,
" blame not the pious inſtitutions of our holy
' church, ſanctified by the obſervance of
" many ages; nor impiouſly arraign the myſ-
" terious decrees of Providence, which often
" produces good from evil. This ſacred
" Edifice has been conſecrated, like many
" others, by our pious anceſtors, for pur-
" poſes honourable to Heaven, and uſeful
" to mankind ; theſe hoſpitable doors are ever
" open to diſtreſs; and the chief object of our
" care is, to diſcover and relieve it. This
" holy manſion has long been an aſylum
" againſt the oppreſſion of human laws,
" which drove *thee* from thine home; and,
" but a few days ſince, *thou* thyſelf bleſſed
" an inſtitution which ſaved the wretched
" *Matilda*, periſhing with madneſs. Nay,
" at this very moment, its mercy ſhelters
" from the hands of juſtice, a murderer ! yet
" thy preſumption dares deny its general
" uſe,

" ufe, from thine own fenfe of partial in-
" convenience, and execrate monaftic inftitu-
" tions, becaufe by a feparation of the fexes,
" lewdnefs and fenfuality are checked : but
" know, fhort-fighted youth, that the world
" will not remain unpeopled, becaufe a *few*
" of its members confecrate their lives to
" *holy meditation*; nor fhall the human fpe-
" cies become extinct, becaufe *Albert* and
" *Matilda* cannot be united, to propagate a
" race of infidels and murderers." ' I ftop-
" ped, for I perceived the gentle *Albert* was
' touched with my rebuke; and falling on his
' knees, he cried in the emphatic words of
' Scripture, " Father! I have finned againft
" Heaven, and in thy fight." " It is enough,
" my fon, (I replied), and now I will com-
" paffionate your fituation ; I will do more,
" for tho' I cannot detain *Matilda* longer than
" till fhe is well enough to be removed ; yet
" in that time (if Heaven approve my endea-
" vours) I may contribute to your happinefs,
" by interceding with her father, and fhould
" I fail in the attempt, this roof, which thy
" hafty paffion has profaned, fhall yet be a
" refuge to thee from defpair; and I will
" ftrive to raife thy thoughts above the
" trifling

" trifling difappointments of a tranfitory
" world."

' I could not wait the reply of *Albert*,
' (faid the Prior) being at this time called
' out to welcome the arrival of a ftranger,
' who they faid was dangeroufly ill; this
' proved to be no other than the wounded
' *Conrad*. He, in few words, explained the
' motive of his vifit, telling me, that imme-
' diately after the rencounter, dreading *that*
' *awful prefence in which no fecret is concealed*,
' and to which he apprehended he was fum-
' moned by his own fword in the injured
' hand of *Albert*, he had vowed (if Heaven
' would grant him life) to repair the wrongs
' he had committed. He had already exe-
' cuted a deed, refigning all the fortune of
' her father in favour of *Matilda*; he had de-
' clared his guilty commerce with *Therefa*,
' that fhe might repent, or fuffer punifh-
' ment; he had paid all the debts of *Albert*,
" and juftified his character to the world;
' and, finally, he had refolved to implore
' the prayers of myfelf, and the venerable fa-
' thers of this houfe, to make him worthy of
' becoming one of our holy order; that if he
' lived, he might be ufeful; or if he died, he
' might be happy.'

THE

THE Prior then concluded this interesting narrative, by saying, that *Albert* and *Matilda* were united, and are still blessed in each other's virtues, improved by difficulties thus surmounted; that *Theresa* had too far profaned the laws of Heaven to have any confidence in religion, and died by her own hands; but that *Conrad* recovered slowly from his wound, and, after living many years an honour to the order he professed, he died in peace: the faithful dog (he said) was the favourite companion of *Albert* and *Matilda*, who had begged him from the convent, and encouraged him to pursue his task of discovering travellers who had lost their way, but whom he now brought to the hospitable mansion of this virtuous pair.

HE then briefly hinted arguments in favour of monastic institutions; yet liberally allowing that the religion of his country might in certain points be wrong, and knowing me to be a Protestant, I suppose he acknowledged more than I ought in justice to his candour to relate. For this reason I have purposely suppressed the name and situation of his convent; but I shall ever remember these words, with which he finished this discourse: " TRUE RELIGION (said he) howsoever it

" may

" may vary in outward ceremonies, or ar-
" ticles of faith, will always teach you to do
" good, to love and help each other; it will
" teach you, that no ſin, however ſecret,
" can long remain concealed; and that when
" the world and all its vanities have palled
" the ſated appetite, you muſt ſeek refuge in
" conſcious innocence, or a ſincere repent-
" ance. Then, no matter whether you chuſe
" a *convent* for retirement, or *commune with*
" *your own heart upon your bed, and be ſtill.*"

N U M-

N U M B E R XXXIII.

THE preceding Tale of the FRIAR AND HIS DOG was firſt communicated to a Brotherhood who call themſelves the

College of United Friars:

Or, SOCIETY *for the* PARTICIPATION *of* USEFUL KNOWLEDGE.

THIS eſtabliſhment, which has been inſtituted only a few years in a large manufacturing city*, is founded on the moſt liberal principles. No conſiderations of rank or fortune

* NORWICH.

fortune have any weight in the choice of its members; but a certain degree of proficiency, either in literature, in the arts, or in some species of elegant or useful knowledge, is a neceſſary qualification in every candidate for admiſſion into the Society; in which (as in moſt others) there are certain forms and regulations known only to the Brotherhood, but among ſuch as are more publicly divulged are the following, viz.

THAT their periodical meetings (called Chapters) are held in a room fitted up and furniſhed with great ſimplicity and elegance, like the refectory of a convent; where all the members, who are called *Friars*, or BROTHERS, are dreſſed in the habit of ſome monaſtic order. If Curioſity ſhould aſk, " Why the Friars are cloathed like Monks?" it may be anſwered, " For the ſame reaſon " that *Free Maſons* wear white leather " aprons."

SOME, who do not remember the old adage of " *Cucullus non facit Monachum*," will annex ideas of religion to the habit of a friar: but theſe muſt have been very ſuperficial obſervers of mankind, or they would ſometimes have diſcovered under the frock and tonſure as great liberality of ſentiment, as under a

laced

laced coat or a tye-wig. The only *Article of Faith* infifted upon by this Proteftant College is, to believe, "that there may be vir-"tuous and able men of every Religion, and "of every Party:" further than this, the rules of the Society abfolutely forbid all difcourfe refpecting Religion or Politics.

WITH the robes of each order are fuppofed to be put on *Meeknefs, Honour, Benevolence, Brotherly Love,* and *Charity,* in its univerfal fenfe. To each garment (though peculiarly diftinguifhed) belongs the fingular virtue of conferring *Equality*; and doing away all diftinction betwixt the moft opulent citizen and the moft indigent mechanic, whofe fkill, genius or abilities, may have entitled him to a feat in the

College of United Friars.

IT is by the confent of this Society that the preceding Tale is now printed, as it was originally delivered by a *non-refident* member to a full Chapter. The uncommon appearance of the fcene, and habits of the auditors, added greatly to the pathetic and folemn effect of the narrative, which, on that occafion, was made to conclude with thefe words:

 " THE

' THE venerable Father, after enumerat-
' ing the usual arguments in favour of mo-
' naſtic inſtitutions, pauſed a while; then,
' with more than common energy, he de-
' clared, " *Methinks my prophetic eye foreſees*
" *a period not far diſtant, when, in your native*
" *iſland, generous* BRITON! *a College of* FRIARS
" *ſhall be eſtabliſhed, in which the advantages of*
" *conventual meetings ſhall be preſerved, diveſted*
" *of their inconveniencies. And while the* BRO-
" THERS *of this new Order revere the memory*
" *of thoſe departed Monks, who, by total ſe-*
" *cluſion from the world, preſerved Literature*
" *in the moſt barbarous ages; they ſhall in that*
" *enlightened period, mix with the world, and*
" *only meet in their College occaſionally, for the*
" *increaſe and* PARTICIPATION OF USEFUL
" KNOWLEDGE."

THIS concluſion, which ſo immediately
appropriated the Tale to the Society, was
received with unbounded applauſe by all
preſent: and one Brother, whoſe eye had
gliſtened with satisfaction during many parts
of the narrative, delivered to the relater the
following elegant compliment, written without heſitation in the moment of ſenſibility
and approbation; which, as an extempore, is
truly beautiful:

" WHEN

" WHEN FANCY tells her tender tale,
" And PASSION fwells her gentle gale,
" Warm beats the ftrong impaffion'd heart,
" And pours a tear, that knows no art.

" 'TWAS done!—Fair FANCY told her tale,
" Our bofoms fwell'd with PASSION's gale;
" TRUTH touch'd the ftrong impaffion'd heart,
" And PITY blefs'd one FRIAR's art."

THE author of this delicate compliment
has promifed to contribute fome Effays,
which encourages the Editor of this little
volume to look forward to a continuation of
his labours at fome future period: but it is
an act of juftice to the Society here introduced to the Public, to declare, that no other
member of it, except the relater of the Friar's
Tale, has in any degree contributed to this
book, nor was the idea of fuch a publication
known to them; but, fhould they think
proper to lend their affiftance, jointly or in-
dividually, what may not be expected from
VARIETY in a fecond volume!

THE hopes from a combination of literary
talents have too often been difappointed, and
promifes of great fupport have frequently

                    ended

ended in very trifling affistance: but it has feldom happened, that fo elegant an excufe has been made for non-performance, as in the following lines. They are part of a letter from a gentleman at Cambridge, in anfwer (by return of poft) to one inclofing the *Hiftory of Tarempou and Scrinda.*

"How could you imagine that an inhabitant of Cambridge could have any thing to do with VARIETY?

"THE willowy CAM no *various* fcenery
        knows:
"Thro' level fields the lazy river flows;
"No mountain dares invade his dull domain,
"Or bind his waters with a rocky chain;
"Ages on ages have beheld him creep
"In ftupid filence to the diftant deep.
"Is this the ftream whofe favour'd banks
        along
"The raptur'd Poet chaunts immortal fong?
"Ah! rather, on the fleep-inducing ftream
"Propt on a bunch of fedge fhall DULLNESS
        dream!
"Or waking hammer out one leaden line,
"And deem herfelf infpir'd, and call the verfe
        divine!

"BUT

" But thee, my friend, what different scenes
    invite,
" Whom sweet VARIETY shall still delight!
" When gentle MAY arrives, as soon she must;
" And *Hare*-(thy spacious)-*street* is fill'd with
    dust;
" I see my friend by Contemplation led,
" Where DRIBBLE gurgles o'er his gravelly
    bed,
" Beneath some shadowing beech behold him
    stand,
" No pliant angle trembling in his hand;
" Superior views his active mind employ;
" Creative Fancy gives a higher joy.
" No tench, 'tis true, nor perch by him is
    caught,
" But many a comic, many a moral thought,
" That sweet relief to sorrow can impart,
" Correct the temper, or amend the heart.

" HAD I the pencil that thy LAMA's drew,
" The arduous task with pleasure I'd pursue;
" VARIETY might then unfold her charms,
" And sweetly smiling take me to her arms.
" But I," &c. &c. &c.

THE Editor having partly made a discovery
of one contributor to this collection, would
be glad to satisfy the curiosity which every

                    reader

reader feels, of becoming acquainted with the several authors of the other Essays; but this at present is not permitted. He may, however, mention the occasion on which the Tale in Nrs. 15 and 16 was written. It had been asserted, that no narrative could be rendered interesting, which was founded on *love at first sight*. This assertion the author controverted, and supported his opinion by producing a Tale founded on a passion between *two lovers who had never seen each other*. How far he has succeeded the Public are now to decide; but some allowance should be made for the *novelty* and *difficulty* of the attempt.

THE same allowance may also be claimed for the Essay signed PHILOPUN, at whose request the second motto is inserted from HORACE.

" Nullius addictus jurare in verba magistri."

" Not bound to swear by any teacher's rules."

THERE are also a few Essays on more serious subjects, which may be thought to require an apology, as in some degree departing from the declaration by which those

topics

topics were pronounced to be inadmiſſible in this collection.

GENERAL Politics and *univerſal* Religion were never intended to be excluded from theſe moral Eſſays; for it ſhould be remembered, that thoſe who endeavour to ſeparate *Religion* and *Morality*, are alike enemies to the true intereſts of ſociety, whether they recommend one or the other *ſingly*: and it is the duty of the periodical Eſſayiſt to notice the moſt prevalent abſurdities of the times in which he lives.

IT ſeems to be the faſhion or folly of the preſent age, to know no medium in matters of *Religion*; and ſhe is equally in danger of being deſtroyed by her friends and enemies: for, while the philoſophic Infidel denies her influence in the affairs of life, the enthuſiaſtic Believer perceives her operation in the moſt trifling concerns of his own.— Degrading the DIVINE PROVIDENCE, by notions of partiality for certain opinions, and confining the benevolence of Heaven to a very few individuals, who are as mad as himſelf. Nothing can more aptly or forcibly deſcribe the ſentiments of theſe narrow-minded bigots, both with reſpect to GOD

and

and man, than the following lines, which
are quoted from memory, without recollecting from whence they are taken; thefe enthufiafts reprefent the DEITY as

> ——————" A Being cruel and fevere,
> " And Man a wretch by his command fent
> here,
> " In funfhine for a while to take a turn,
> " Only to dry, and make him fit to burn.""

Such unjuft, unmerciful, and impious fentiments cannot be too ftrenuoufly oppofed, for
they are directly contrary to the fpirit of that
religion which fhould bring " peace on earth,
" and good-will towards men."

ANY endeavours, therefore, to infpire more
liberal notions of Chriftianity, can give no
offence but to thofe miftaken zealots, which
will allow of no *variety* in the opinions of
mankind; and who, from their little knowledge of what muft neceffarily be the cafe in
this world, feem to have paffed all their lives
in the planet which LUNATICUS defcribes:
for, whatever may be the fate of this little
volume, or its feveral authors, the world

itfelf

itſelf will finiſh, before either in opinions,
in characters, in faſhions, in literature, in
politics, or even in religion itſelf, there can
ever be an

END of VARIETY.

E R R A T A.

Page 10, *line* 25, *for* delight,   *read* day-light.
    48, —— 2, —— whoever, —— who never.
    58, —— 24, —— kind, —— hind.
    62, —— 19, —— learn, —— earn.
    120, —— 10, —— medicines, —— medicine.
    124, —— 13, —— repled, —— replied.
    145, —— 3, —— warm, —— warms.
    156, —— 13, —— pou, —— you.
    157, —— 12, —— the, —— then.
    173, —— 10, —— rude elbows, —— butchers' trays.
    243, —— 9, —— confined, —— conferred.

www.ingramcontent.com/pod-product-compliance
Lightning Source LLC
Chambersburg PA
CBHW031046120726
47905CB00007B/2325